The Prince of Santa Fe

The Law Wranglers

Ron Schwab

Uplands Press

OMAHA, NEBRASKA

Uplands Press
1401 S 64th Avenue
Omaha, NE 68106
www.uplandspress.com

Ordering Information:
Quantity sales. Special discounts are available on quantity purchases by corporations, associations, and others. For details, contact the "Special Sales Department" at the address above.

Uplands Press / Ron Schwab -- 1st ed.
ISBN 978-1-943421-74-9

Lockwood

The Accidental Sheriff
Beware a Pale Horse
Trouble

Sioux Sunrise
Paint the Hills Red
Grit
Cut Nose
The Long Walk
Coldsmith
Ghost of the Guadalupe
Bushwa

The Prince of Santa Fe

The Law Wranglers

Chapter 1

JESSICA CHANDLER WELCOMED the warm caress of the midmorning sun on her face as she stepped onto the boardwalk outside the Teatro Santa Fe. She savored spring here, the purple aster and butterfly weed budding now with a few displaying early flowers, and other plant life returning from winter napping as well.

Snow-capped mountains towered above the foothills that surrounded the bowl of near desert where Santa Fe commerce was carried on. Those caps would begin melting soon if they had not already, and in another month, no more than two, the Rio Grande to the west and its feeding creeks and streams would begin to run banks-full of water precious as gold.

Jessica loved this town and its exotic setting. She had lived here over ten years now, and this is where she hoped to die, preferably much later than sooner. She had much to do yet with her life as owner and director of the Teatro Santa Fe. The theater she had established in a small, abandoned Catholic church building was the embodiment of her dream.

She paused a minute. She had caught sight of that man, the skinny, pale man with the black mustache wearing a Mexican sombrero. He had disappeared into the San Francisco Street entrance to the Exchange Hotel dining room, but she was certain he had been watching her again. He was well-dressed in a gray suit and string bow tie. Apart from the sombrero, his clothes were Anglo-style garments, and the hue of his skin did not suggest Spanish ancestry, not that it mattered to her. She did not take kindly to anyone following her.

She shrugged and continued her journey to her lawyer's office. She had recently purchased the last shares held by the investors who financed the purchase and remodeling of the theater, freeing up funds that would allow her to indulge in a few luxuries now and then. She had lived frugally, almost miserly, over these past years, pouring every surplus dollar into her theater.

Now that Santa Fe had railroad access, she was confident she could attract traveling performers and shows more easily. They seemed to be hungry for new opportunities in the west granted by the transportation links now available. Regardless, she would continue to fill scheduling gaps with local performances where her thespians took to the stage for the sheer fun and glory of those moments in front of an audience. With no salaries to pay, those productions were quite profitable, even with lower attendance and reduced admission prices. Of course, she admitted, filling her own need to perform was no small part of her motivation.

Since her early teenage years, she had been an actress. Raised in a St. Louis orphanage, she had run away at age fifteen and latched on to small acting parts with troupes that came to town, sometimes playing two or three roles during the same performance, binding her ample breasts when necessary to play male characters.

It was the latter ability that landed her the leading male role as Mazeppa in a play based upon Lord Byron's poem of the same name. The male actor who was to perform the role had deserted the troupe and left abruptly with no notice. Her performance had yielded standing ovations, the audience unaware that she was a young woman.

Based upon her talent and versatility, she quickly grabbed a permanent job with the traveling troupe. Although Francis Collette, the troupe's manager, was a generation older, she had eventually married him for convenience's sake.

Poor Francis, he would have loved being a part of the Teatro Santa Fe. In addition to management duties, he was also as fine an actor as he was an inept lover. If she had remained faithful during their marriage, she might yet be able to identify as a virtuous woman, but a parade of male actors over the years had lured her from that notion. A leading man in Romeo and Juliet had awakened a sleeping animal within her, and fidelity died that night.

She had liked Francis well enough, and he tolerated her affairs without complaint. She suspected that the dearth of female performers available to travel with the troupe from town to town across the country played no small part in his tolerance. Later, she learned that his true affection was for the company's owner and fellow actor, George Beeson.

Comanche, however, abruptly ended that chapter of her life. She had been aboard a stagecoach headed for a week of performances in Santa Fe when a small war party attacked, scalping, mutilating, and killing every member of the troupe except one. She alone had survived thanks to the man she was on her way to visit, Josh Rivers. Josh had been riding near the Cimmaron Cutoff that day when he saw the smoke from the burning stagecoach and investigated. He killed one of the warriors, and the others departed. Eventually, he had taken her to the company's original destination, and she chose to plant roots. She took Josh as a lover for a time, but when Jael, now his wife and a law partner, entered his life, that ended, and they both moved on without regret.

She stopped in front of the Rivers & Sinclair law offices on the Plaza. Circumstances dictated that she consult with her lawyer and the man she trusted above all others.

Chapter 2

LINDA DE LA Cruz entered Josh Rivers's private office after a single warning tap on the door. Josh looked up from the file on his desktop. The petite Mexican woman was a treasure he would not allow to escape. Fluent in English and Spanish, competent in Pueblo, she was frequently pressed into interpreter's duties, aside from being his personal secretary and the firm's office manager.

"Jessica has arrived. I trust you remember that you have an appointment with her?"

She knew he would not forget an appointment with Jessica. He could not imagine any man forgetting an appointment with Jessica. It was not just the woman's beauty. Her blunt, no-nonsense personality generally left an impression on most who encountered her. He stood. "I'll step out and escort her in."

"Not necessary." It was Jessica, who had glided into the office behind Linda de la Cruz. "I escorted myself."

Josh looked at Linda, who was already disappearing through the doorway, closing the door behind her. He turned back to the woman with jade-green eyes and flowing black hair who was already moving toward him. He stepped out from behind the desk and accepted the hug and soft kiss on his cheek that he had anticipated. It was very quick and not unchaste, but he still remembered Jael's questioning look the first time she had seen Jessica embrace him when greeting them before a performance at the Teatro Santa Fe.

He had never discussed his prior relationship with Jessica with his wife. But her look told him she knew, and now on such occasions, Jael just smiled and seemed to enjoy his discomfiture.

He pulled a chair out in front of his desk and seated his client before he returned to his own swivel chair. "Well, Jessica, I'm surprised to see you so soon. It hasn't been a week since we settled on my interest in the theater."

"You were the last. I own one hundred per cent now, free and clear. I am grateful to you and others who backed me, but it's a nice feeling to know that it's truly mine."

"You should be proud of that. It's a great asset to our town. I talked to some of the investors, and we would have turned our shares over to you eventually anyway."

"I don't want to owe anybody. I wouldn't have taken charity."

"Well, I'm just glad it worked out for you. Now, what's on today's agenda?"

"I am enceinte."

"Enceinte? I don't know more than a dozen words of French, but are you telling me you are with child?"

"My, I knew there was a reason I had you for my lawyer. You are so astute."

Sarcasm flowed naturally from Jessca's mouth with ease. "I think you made your appointment at the wrong office. Doctor Micah Rand's clinic is about three blocks east of here."

"I will visit Micah in due course. I assume he is still sleeping with your partner, Amanda Sinclair?"

"That is neither your concern nor mine. Now, let's put the games aside. What do you need a lawyer for?"

"You don't seem too surprised that I am with child."

"Well, I admit I was taken aback some. I thought you might be past that age." He regretted the words the instant they slipped out, and the sparks in her eyes confirmed it.

"Just how old do you think I am?"

He figured she surpassed his age by a half dozen or so years. That would place her somewhere a bit on either side of forty-two years. "I would guess you at about thirty-five."

"You are lying. You pretty much know my life's history, and you have likely figured close. I am forty-three, and it is not unheard of for women that age to have a child. But, as you well know, I have had a few opportunities over the years, and I long ago assumed I could not."

"Uh, congratulations, then." He knew she was currently seeing Charles Hanover, a man who called himself "the Prince of Santa Fe."

"I do know how to dispose of this inconvenience, but the child is my own flesh and blood. I will carry the child and bear it and be a mother like no other."

She would certainly be a mother like no other. "Then I am truly happy for you, Jessica."

"Now, the questions for my lawyer. I have not told the father yet, but by my count I should be approaching three months, and I can tell the baby is beginning to show some. He will guess it very soon. The father is the Prince of Santa Fe. The baby will be a prince or princess."

"I am sorry to inform you that royalty is not recognized in this country. Your child will not inherit a title and receive no special privileges because of it."

"But royal blood still might have meaning to some folks."

"Europe maybe. Some places back east among the wealthy class, I suppose. Don't count on it here." He was reluctant to tell her that her prince was considered something of a joke in Santa Fe, but her current romance tended to blind her to reality sometimes.

"Anyway, I am certain the prince is the father. As you know, I have had several lovers over the years, but I always see just one man exclusively till I tire of him or life sends us different ways, as was our case. I do not want my child born a bastard."

Josh said, "Then you must marry the prince. Will he be willing to take a wife?"

"Possibly, at least for a time, until one of us has had enough of the other."

"I see. I don't know much about the prince beyond representing some clients who sold property to him. He must have an enormous amount of money invested in that castle, and I know his land holdings are extensive. My guess is that he will be quite wary of putting any of it at risk in a marriage."

"I am certain of that. And I do not want to chance losing my theater. If he chooses to marry me, is there some way I can protect the theater and assure him that I have no claim upon his properties?"

"Yes, there are agreements that can provide protections. He possibly could not evade support of the child, and in case of divorce, many courts grant the husband priority in awarding physical custody of a child---the husband's right to the child's services in providing support. In short, you might be at a disadvantage in keeping your child in case of divorce."

"I can't accept that risk. Can't we have an agreement about that before marriage?"

"I am not aware of any of those in New Mexico. I can do some research on the subject from other jurisdictions, but, regardless, I doubt if I would be able to give you much reassurance. The law on child custody is nebulous and ever-changing. If you entered into an agreement today, there is nothing to guarantee that a court in the future would not invalidate it."

"We can't vote, and the men have priority to custody of our children. Women are just a step above slavery in this country. That will change someday."

"I have two female law partners including my wife. You don't think I haven't heard that before? I didn't make the suffrage laws. Don't blame me."

"Humph. Well, I've got to deal with what is. I don't think I will be looking to get married. What do you think the chances are that I could be married to one man for twenty years?"

Slim to none, he thought, but did not say it. He just shrugged.

"Yeah, I know what you're thinking. I intend to say nothing to the good prince until he figures it out for himself. Maybe I will tell him I'm having another man's child."

"Be wary of this guy. He's about finished building that castle in the hills just outside of town. We can see it from our little ranch. It's an eyesore on the landscape, but he's spending a lot of money. I have no idea where that comes from."

"Family money, Charles says. He claims to be from the Hanover family, a line of royal blood that has connections throughout Europe."

"Queen Victoria is from the House of Hanover. I read once that the family has its roots in Germany. They assumed the English throne in the early 1700s when parliament passed a law declaring that only Protestants could ascend to the throne. That ended the Stuart line because they were Catholic. I don't understand how this all takes place, but if your prince were of great importance or in the line of succession, I suspect he could live with more luxury in England."

"Perhaps he has an adventurous spirit."

Josh was skeptical. "I suppose that's possible."

Jessica said, "Well, you have given me some things to ponder. One more thing..."

"Yes?"

"I think a man may be following me, but I can't say for certain."

"A stranger, I gather."

"Yes. If I knew him, I would take him to task, but it's possible my imagination is at work. My sightings could be coincidences."

"Can you describe him?"

"He wears a sombrero and has a black mustache, but any Mexican resemblance ends there. Very pale face and wears a suit and dresses like an Anglo otherwise. Skinny, much shorter than you. I couldn't make out his facial features very well, but I would guess him to be in his early forties. Erect bearing like someone who might have served in the military."

Josh stood a few inches over six feet, so many men would be shorter. "You are very observant."

"The theater does that. I evaluate everyone based on how they might appear on stage. I am constantly assigning roles to people in my mind. You have been cast as the perfect leading man on several occasions. I almost asked you once but learned that you and Jael were leaving for the Comanche reservation near Fort Sill and would be absent for a month or two."

"I'm not an actor."

"Oh, yes you are. You just don't know it. Some time I will coerce you onto a stage, perhaps cast your wife as leading lady and get her on my side."

"You can be devious. I will be on guard. Now, about the man you suspect is following you, does he look threatening? I haven't noticed anyone with that description in town lately."

"It's just been two days. He doesn't wear a holstered pistol on a gun belt, but that doesn't mean he doesn't have one secreted under his coat. I'm more curious than worried."

"You tell me if you get more concerned. Do you mind if I mention this to Jael and Danna?"

"That is fine with me. I prefer they not know about the expected child yet but anything else is fine. I would certainly like to learn more about the prince if they might be helpful."

"Yes, the prince. I think we should learn more about him."

Chapter 3

CHARLES HANOVER STOOD in the uppermost room of the watchtower at what he called "Hanover Castle," a stuccoed, adobe replica of a European castle drawing he had found in a book. Alas, he had no moat surrounding it, but the parapet walls that stood no less than ten feet high offered ample protection from attacks. He had been attracted to that idea to defend against raiding Indians, only to learn later that Indian raids were no longer a threat.

The tribes were increasingly moving to reservations, and Fort Marcy in Santa Fe had recently been reactivated by the Army. With Fort Union less than a half day's ride to the east, Apache and other warrior bands no longer troubled folks residing within twenty miles of Santa Fe. Still, he had potential enemies who might pursue the secrets he held here, and he was comforted by the notion that his hired guns could fight off a small army from the parapets if necessary.

Charles Hanover was born Egbert Hopkins in Boston just short of fifty years earlier. His wealthy family saw to an elite education, and he might have graduated from Harvard Law School had he not been expelled for masterminding and profiting from a sophisticated operation that produced papers for students and acquired examination questions from blackmailed professors whose private lives his spies tracked. By that time, he was needing money because his father's vast investments in the South were disappearing because of the war, leaving the family nearly destitute.

Facing conscription by the Union Army, Egbert Hopkins disappeared and emerged in Illinois as Charles Hanover. The Hanover name had been adopted because of Queen Victoria's lineage, but he had not installed himself as a prince until ten years later when he learned that his claimed royal blood could open many doors. He had never been to Europe, of course, and did not know that much about the royal families, but the men he dealt with knew less than nothing about such things.

Since embarking upon his career as a royal, Hanover carried himself erect with his head held high, thinking of himself as a lofty presence although his height was the average man's five feet, nine inches. His longish, dark brown hair was kept carefully trimmed just above the shoulders and not a hair wandered from his mustache and goatee. He was sturdily constructed, but he had not allowed his body to go to fat. There was a deceptive innocence and seductiveness in his pale blue eyes that women seemed to like, and he had not permitted that attribute to go to waste.

Sometimes, he had to remind himself that his royal blood was a sham. After all, he felt like a prince and was likely wealthier than most via his alliances with bank robbers, rustlers, kidnappers and the like. He also had recently embarked on using his resources to acquire legitimate businesses, and he aspired to purchasing banking and other interests in Santa Fe, as well as ranching operations over the next several years. It was time to remove the risks of working outside the law. He had decided to honor Santa Fe as the capital of his kingdom.

There was a rap on the door behind him and he turned away from the window. "Who is it?"

"Paddy."

"Come in." Paddy O'Meara was Prince Charles's Knight Grand Cross, his second in command who issued orders to all the knight commanders scattered about the West.

Paddy pushed the door open and waddled into the small tower room. Unlike the prince, he did not display the storybook image of a knight grand cross. A few inches shorter than his prince, Paddy was rotund and fleshy, a thick red beard hiding jowls that made him appear neckless. He also refused to participate in the royalty game. He was a no-nonsense former Army sergeant with a quick mind and sense of how to make things happen. Hanover could not afford to lose him, so tolerance of certain insubordinations was mandatory.

"Trouble, Boss," Paddy said. "According to our contact there, a woman at the Second National Bank has been asking questions about your business, looking at the accounts."

"A woman? Do you mean a bank clerk?"

"I mean a bank officer. The first vice president."

"I can't believe they'd let a female be an officer. What kind of a bank is that? Maybe we ought to take our money out."

"Sorry to say she's Irish, too. At least her pa must have been. Her handle's Rylee O'Brian. Must have got an Irish brain anyhow. Can't be out of her early twenties, and she holds down an important bank job."

Hanover saw no humor in the remark. "The boss must be bedding her, or she's got something on him."

"Willi Spiegelberg runs the bank for the family. Him and his four brothers own the bank, you know. They started the bank in a corner of their mercantile store till they outgrowed it. And the store keeps spreading out, too."

"They'd better enjoy it, because in five years' time, I intend to own it all or crowd them down to nothing."

"My contact says that this O'Brian woman's head works like a machine when it comes to numbers. She's head cashier and bookkeeping supervisor at the bank as part of her duties. I don't know what she's up to. What would she find in your accounts there?"

"Not a damn thing. Most of our money is in the vault here. You know that. I put just enough money in the banks to be respectable. Maybe I ought to borrow some money, talk to this woman about it. It would give me an opportunity to ask a few questions, maybe pick up a hint of what she's after or say some things that might satisfy her curiosity."

"You don't need anybody's loan, but I think you're on to something. I'll tell the contact to keep us up to date. If you plan to sink your roots here, I say it's best not to start any killings close by. You might even want to re-think the notion of robbing the Second National."

"We'll see. If your Irish friend turns out to be a problem, she might find herself a hostage in a bank robbery."

Paddy shook his head doubtfully. "Don't like it."

"I'll talk with this O'Brian woman within the next week. For the next few days, I've got to stay close to be sure the builders get the residence section of the castle finished. The duchess and young prince and princesses will arrive in less than a month."

"I don't think that's a problem, but you ain't got furniture."

"The duchess wants to tend to that personally. There is a furniture store with the funeral parlor in town, and the Spiegelberg Mercantile seems to have a nice selection. I have furnished the royal suite myself with purchases brought by railroad from the East. But we should spend most of our money locally, demonstrate that we are loyal residents of the community. I will make some personal calls this week and arrange for credit with all the merchants. It is time to be a part of the community."

"Suit yourself. Remember, in two weeks we've got the five foremen coming in to report and turn in profits. They'll be wanting new jobs. We need to talk before we meet with them."

"Knight commanders, not foremen. Of course, we should talk, but I'm sure you already have plans laid out."

Chapter 4

RYLEE O'BRIAN SAT in her private office at the Second National Bank of Santa Fe, her sable hair cascading over the shoulders of her gray jacket. She always dressed conservatively at the bank, usually wearing a high-necked white blouse to match a gray, black or dark blue suit. Not quite twenty-three years old and a woman, she felt it important that she appear businesslike. Over ninety per cent of her customers were male, and the majority were middle-aged or beyond.

The office was private only insofar as conversations were concerned since a window facing the lobby and another on a side wall revealed the occupants—except for the few occasions when she elected to close the curtains. This morning she was meeting with Charles Hanover, the man who had built the castle in the hills not more than a few miles from the small ranch where she resided with Josh and Jael Rivers and their son, Michael.

Hanover, impeccably attired in a striped suit and a black tie held with a diamond stud, had just taken a chair and was sitting in front of her desk, tossing his eyes uneasily about the room. He said, "Do you suppose you might close the curtains? I would prefer privacy."

She stood, "Certainly. I can do that." The windows provided light to the room that otherwise relied upon an oil lamp for lighting. They also offered a two-way security measure. They permitted the occupant to supervise employee activity in the bank, and they assured that other employees would see if something untoward such as an assault on a bank officer or robbery attempt was taking place. She did not see Hanover as a threat, not personally anyhow. Monied people generally hired others to carry out any law breaking on their behalves.

With the curtains closed, Rylee turned up the lamp to brighten the now dusky office. "Now, Mister Hanover, how may I help you?"

"As you are no doubt aware, I am an account holder with your bank and have a fair number of transactions on my accounts."

"Yes, you have been banking here for over a year now, and we do appreciate your business."

"I anticipate making significant land purchases in the northern half of the territory over the next several years. I own a considerable amount of property clear of any mortgage debt, but I will require loans to make some of the future purchases. I would like to establish credit with your bank, so I can count on a loan when I am negotiating with sellers. You can often obtain some price reduction if you are able to offer cash without any conditions, such as loan acquisition, attached."

"I'm certain we could make a commitment for a fixed amount once you provide a financial statement."

"A financial statement?"

"Yes. A listing of all your properties located in New Mexico that you would have available to mortgage—along with current liabilities, of course. We would confirm valuations with our own appraisers and arrange title searches on all the properties to confirm that they are free of liens and mortgages."

"You wouldn't trust my figures?"

"We would take your numbers into consideration, but we are a conservative bank, Mister Hanover. We are looking to make loans, but we're very conscious of the obligation to protect our customers' deposits."

"That is admirable, I suppose. I haven't encountered this before. I have been fortunate to be born to a family of some wealth, and I am proud to say I have built upon what my ancestors passed on to me."

"You are a credit to your family then. Many fritter away their inheritances. I have heard that you are related to the British royal family."

"That is true, but I am several cousins removed from the queen. My ancestors belong to another branch."

"The Germans, perhaps?"

"Uh, yes, of course."

"But not directly descended from George Louis, elector of Hanover?"

Hanover's face reddened, and he was obviously flustered. "My family came to America several generations ago, so I do not know many relatives in Germany."

"I was referring to the George Louis who became King George the first of Britain in the early 1700s, the ancestor of Queen Victoria."

"Oh, of course, that George Louis. I am not a direct descendant. My ancestor would have been a younger brother, as I recall."

It was not her job to embarrass customers, certainly not to chase them away, so she quickly shifted the conversation back to business. "About a loan, it is more common for someone to contact us after they have identified a property for purchase. If the borrower has funds to pay a portion of the price, the bank will loan as much as sixty percent and take a first mortgage as security. But you wish advance approval for loans for one hundred percent of the price on properties yet to be identified. In that instance, we would require mortgages on other properties sufficient to cover the amount above what we would otherwise loan."

"Well, if I decide I want to do business with your people, I will have my accountants start compiling a list. I'm sure I have considerably more assets than needed to secure any loans."

"Just try to place a realistic value on the assets. On farm and ranch lands, an on-site visit might not even be necessary for our appraisals. Certainly, we would try to act quickly in arriving at a figure for what we call a line of credit."

"Well, you have given me something to consider. It will probably be a few weeks before I decide how I am going to proceed."

He stood to leave, Rylee rose from her own chair and went around the desk to offer her hand, which was received with a limp response. "I hope we can do business, Mister Hanover. I would be pleased to work with you, or if you prefer, the bank has another loan officer you might be more comfortable with." She knew that some men did not trust women with financial matters, and she did not have time to concern herself with their biases.

"You will be hearing from me, I'm sure," Hanover said.

Rylee watched as Hanover turned away and strutted down the corridor between the tellers' stations and desks that led to the exit before donning his round-crowned bowler and stepping out onto the new concrete walk in front of the bank. She did not like the man, but it was not necessary for her to like customers to do business with them. Her job was to produce profits for the Spiegelberg family, a daunting challenge for most enterprises, and one she relished. Numbers. Business. She worked more hours than anyone in the bank. And she loved it.

Charles Hanover worried her, though. She had received the unsigned note by mail almost a month earlier, a message scrawled across a plain, yellowish sheet of parchment: Beware of the Hanover prince. He is a fraud, thief and murderer of innocents.

She had taken the message to the bank president Willi Spiegelberg, who had simply said, "It is probably nothing but keep your eyes and ears open. This could be from someone with a personal grudge. Just be wary. Tell me if you learn more."

It was time to speak with Willi again.

Chapter 5

JESSICA CHANDLER ANTICIPATED the prince's visit to her two-room suite at the Exchange Hotel tonight. Wednesday night was their scheduled rendezvous night at the suite, and he generally stayed the night and departed just before dawn. Occasionally, he stopped by for a spontaneous romp, but he never stayed over those nights. She had lived in Santa Fe long enough to know that their intimacy was no secret, but the prince seemed to think he was fooling someone.

He slipped in the back door at night and came up to the second floor via the service stairway just inside. She smiled as she busied herself tidying the room, wondering if the stairway had been installed for such clandestine night visits. The whores routinely used the convenient access.

As usual she was ready for frolicking tonight. Curse or blessing, she had an appetite that could match any man. Her enthusiasm was dampened, however, by the message she must convey to her lover. She had planned to tell him last Wednesday night, only days after her meeting with Josh. She hoped he would share her joy at the prospect of fatherhood, but she did not know him all that well beyond his more than adequate performance as a lover. He was not a man who divulged his secrets in the bedroom.

After six months, it would not be unnatural for a woman to visit the prince's castle, if not for the night at least for an afternoon tour. She certainly had hinted often enough that she would enjoy a glimpse of the residence that the entire populace speculated about. Of course, it was possible she might be living there soon if they came to terms about the child. She had decided that she would consider marriage just to give the baby legitimacy if they could enter into an agreement for her custody in the event of divorce. She would gladly relinquish any claim to his property or support. Josh had advised her of the risks, but she had decided to take the chance.

She had not eaten after she left the theater for the day, wanting to bathe in the hotel ladies' tub room downstairs and freshen up some before her guest's arrival. It occurred to her that the prince had taken her out to dinner only twice, and that was several months ago. When they first met, it was at one of the Teatro Santa Fe's performances, her first attempt at a burlesque production that had been billed for males only. She had imported two entertainers from Denver, one a story-telling comedian, whose tales were on the lewd side if not downright vulgar. The other was a young woman, tall and blonde, who strolled back and forth stark-naked reciting female dialogue from Shakespearean plays. She was pretty enough, expressive and agile—a fine actress—but carried at least two hundred pounds on her five-and-one-half-foot frame. The audience adored her and rendered multiple standing ovations.

Jessica had hired a local Mexican band to perform and recruited Santa Fe saloon girls and more than a few prostitutes to make up a chorus and form a dance line wearing risqué costumes that fell just short of outright nudity. Several young locals from respectable families signed on to perform as well. Jessica had joined the dancers and sung several solos herself. She could not resist the stage.

The burlesque had performed to a packed house the first night, and second and third nights brought standing room only attendance. She had made a lot of money and evidently gained more than a few new theater attendees, because attendance at future traditional shows

were crowded also. She was certain she would do burlesque again and toyed with the idea of a female only
performance. Several so-called respectable ladies had
suggested the idea. She thought it would be fun to see
how many women abandoned their husbands for such a
night.

The prince had attended the first night's performance
and had waited in the lobby to meet her after the crowd
dispersed. His handsome looks and muscular physique
had attracted her instantly, and she wondered what
might be beneath the layers of his expensive wardrobe.
He had congratulated her on the success of the production and praised her own performance as singer and
dancer lavishly. He had also told her she was incredibly
beautiful.

He returned the next night, greeting her again. And
the next night. That was when she invited him to her hotel suite for a drink. They never did get around to having
the drink, but he spent most of the night.

It was nearly eight o'clock when a soft rap on her door
told her that the prince had arrived. She opened it, and
he stepped into the room with that devilish smile on his
face, pushed the door shut, took her in his arms and
pressed his lips to hers. She was naked beneath her silk
robe and could feel his urgency. It was then she realized

he had arrived sans coat and tie. She could not recall ever seeing him without formal attire, except, of course, when he was disrobing for their lovemaking. She also smelled whiskey on this breath. He generally drank little when he was with her, and it surprised her that he had been drinking, although a drink or two was certainly no sin.

He released her, stepped back, and looked at her with pale blue eyes that had a wildness in them. "I can't wait," he said.

"Charles, I'm pleased to accommodate a man in a hurry to start our evening." She took his hand and led him into the bedroom, where the oil lamp was already lit and set low.

She released his hand and slipped out of the silk gown that had covered her nakedness and let it slide down her long legs to the floor before crawling beneath the bedsheets to watch her paramour. The prince sat down on the bed and pulled off his boots. In a matter of minutes, he crawled in bed beside her. Without preliminaries, he took her without a hint of gentleness and obviously no concern for her pleasure. When he rolled away and lay beside her, she could not remain quiet.

"Are you angry about something? You were not forced to visit tonight."

"I wanted you."

"What about what I want?"

"You are a woman. You don't have the same needs."

"I certainly don't need your company when you are like this." She got out of bed, snatched up her robe, and put in on, clutching it tightly about her. "I think you should go back to your damn castle now."

He swung his legs over the side of the bed and looked at her, a silent snarl on his lips signaling his contempt. Should she tell him about the expected child? She knew now she would not marry this man. As she watched him dress, she decided that he should know.

As Hanover prepared to leave, he said, "I will come back when you are in a better mood."

"I doubt if there will be a better mood where you are concerned, but there is something you should be aware of."

"Yes?"

"I am with child."

His eyes narrowed, and he stepped toward her. "You are pregnant? You can't be."

"I didn't think so either, but I am certain of it."

"Are you suggesting I had something to do with this?"

She laughed, "You do know what causes babies, don't you?"

His face reddened, and he glowered at her. "It could be the child of a dozen men I am guessing."

She stepped up and slapped his face sharply. "There have been no other men."

His fist whipped out and hammered her below the right eye. She staggered backward, dizzy from the blow. "Get out of here, you bastard. Now."

"Your child is the real bastard here. It is not mine, and I will not marry you. My wife and children will be joining me here in a few weeks."

"You told me you were not married."

"I lied. And if you make any claim that I fathered this child, I will deny it and see your theater closed. I will not have you embarrass me or my family with this outlandish claim. There are ways to make that baby disappear, and if you don't know how, talk to one of the other whores in town. I suggest you do this soon."

He wheeled and walked out of the bedroom. Jessica did not move until she heard the outer door slam. She ran her fingers gingerly over the burning, tender spot where his fist had struck her. It was starting to swell now, and she would not be a pretty sight tomorrow.

Fortunately, she was committed to no personal performances at the theater anytime soon. In another week, Lydia Thompson, known as the "Queen of Burlesque," would bring her troupe called "British Blondes" for six nights of performances, and with extra make-up she should be presentable for introduction. She was excited by her success in landing this famous lady and expected to draw customers from many miles. To hell with the so-called "Prince of Santa Fe." Life would go on just fine without him.

Jessica conceded that a female confidante would be welcome now, however. She decided to visit Tabitha Rivers Wolf soon.

Chapter 6

"THE PRINCE OF Santa Fe was in my office while you were in Denver, Willi. I thought I should bring you up to date." Rylee had promised to call her mentor, the Second National Bank president, by his first name when she reached the age of twenty-one. That would have been over a year ago, and she still did not feel comfortable addressing her employer in that manner.

"By all means, my dear, please do so."

They were seated in Willi Spiegelberg's office, which was essentially a copy of her own. Spiegelberg was a down-to-earth man in his late fifties who avoided pretense like the plague. He was by nature a kindly man, a widower without children who looked upon Rylee as the daughter he never had.

"He claimed to be interested in loans for purchasing real estate and investment properties. He would like to procure a line of credit, so he doesn't have to look to the bank's approval for every transaction. He was not especially pleased when I explained that he would be required to present a list of assets and that we would have our own appraisals made."

Spiegelberg raked his fingers through wiry salt and paper hair and shrugged. "Which is what we would require of any borrower. We have customers to protect."

Willi Spiegelberg had his eye on a profit as much as the next man but was unfailingly honest and conscious of his responsibilities to his customers and employees. Rylee worshipped this paunchy man who was not a formidable-looking figure, several inches shorter than her own five-feet-nine inches and always attired in white shirt, string bow tie and suit. "Charles Hanover does not see himself as just any customer. He seems to have convinced himself that the lie of his royal blood is true and entitles him to privileges."

"Lie?"

"He knows nothing about the royal family he claims he is descended from and admits he has never been to any of the countries ruled by the Hanover line. He is a fraud. I find Queen Victoria fascinating and have read anything I can find about her and the family. Charles Hanover has not even bothered to educate himself about his so-called relatives. And I think he knows that I am aware of it. His wealth did not come from a royal inheritance, I assure you."

"The warning note tells us we should be cautious in our dealings with Mister Hanover. He might not be a trustworthy borrower, but his lying does not mean he is a dangerous man."

"True enough. But I intend to learn everything I can about this man so we are prepared for any dealings we might have with him."

"That would only be prudent if we should find ourselves doing business with him."

"We have used the Pinkerton Detective Agency's new service on credit checking customers on several occasions. They conduct a national search of public records to see what information turns up. It doesn't involve agents in the field, so it is relatively inexpensive. Would you object to my running Hanover's name through the process?"

"No, I'll leave that to your judgment. Why don't you assign the task to Tabor Britton? Your time is too valuable to spend on such things."

"I guess I could do that. We're not keeping him as busy as I'd like anyway. He seems able to tally numbers and make journal entries well enough, but I don't like his manner when he's on teller duties. He lacks patience in dealing with customers, and I have had complaints that he is occasionally downright crabby."

"You have spoken with him about this?"

"Yes, of course. He blames the customer and then is sullen around me for several days after."

"Well, we hired him because we need another book-keeper. We just try to train people so they can fill in wherever needed in the bank. Remember, Rylee, Tabor is just a boy. He is not yet twenty-five, and this is his first banking experience."

"I would remind you, Willi, that he is older than I am."

"You, my dear, are an exception to every notion I ever had about youth—and women for that matter. I swear you were born without recognizing limitations of age or sex."

She shrugged. Willi Spiegelberg knew only fragments of her back story. She had been forced as a child to grow up fast and to make decisions that most never faced in a lifetime. "I confess that Tabor makes me uneasy for some reason, but I promise that I will be patient with him."

"That's all I ask. I know I hired him while you were in Phoenix helping Mike Goldwater with some problems at his bank. You have the authority to fire Tabor if you decide he will not fit. I would just like to see him given a chance. By the way, that ornery varmint, Mike Goldwater, told me at the bankers' meeting that he would like to hire you away from here. I told him to be prepared for a bidding war and that you would eventually have my job if you stayed on."

She smiled. "I'm not going anywhere, and I cannot imagine taking on your job. Don't worry, I will be patient with Tabor Britton." She stood. "And now I had better get back to work and prove that I am worthy of your kind compliments."

Back in her own office, she pondered her conversation with Willi. He had been so good to her that she had not wanted to argue with him about the merits, or lack of them, of Tabor Britton. She did not like him. He was lazy, impudent and barely competent in her judgment. She would try being patient a bit longer, but she felt his firing within a month or two was inevitable.

Rylee did not like the idea of Britton's participation in the Hanover investigation, but she would not disregard her employer's instructions. That was not her style. She pulled a parchment pad from her desk drawer and began to write a list of questions she wanted the Pinkerton Agency to pursue. Then she summoned Tabor Britton to her office. She figured she was still ultimately responsible for results, and she would not give Britton free rein.

When Britton followed her into the private office, his dark eyes darted back and forth like he was about to be attacked, and when he sat down on the opposite side of her desk, he began tapping his fingers nervously on the desktop. He always behaved this way in her presence, and she could not understand why. She considered herself a congenial person who never raised her voice at bank employees. She tried to treat everyone with respect, even Tabor Britton, although she supposed he could sense she was not fond of him. She conceded that she had a rather serious demeanor, however, and tended not to be a part of the bantering and joking that the staff carried on. Some might have said she was aloof, but she did not sense hostility or dislike among her co-workers.

"Mister Britton," Rylee said, "I have a little project I would like your assistance with."

"Yes, ma'am."

It occurred to her that Britton appeared the proper banker, his brown hair neatly trimmed and pale face clean shaven save for sideburns that dropped to the bottom tips of his ears. He was a man of average height, probably close to her own, always impeccably dressed in a freshly pressed suit. And he was a handsome fellow, although she was not attracted to him.

She handed him two sheets of paper. "I would like to have you contact the Pinkerton Agency regarding investigation of a potential customer. This is not urgent, so I will have you do this by mail. You will find the name and address of our Pinkerton contact on one of the sheets. His name is Carl Chirnside of the Kansas City office."

"So you want me to send this man a letter?"

"Yes, but I want to review it before it goes out. The day after tomorrow would be soon enough. I also want you to send Mister Chirnside a telegram advising him to expect the letter and asking him to advise of any advance payment required. I doubt if that will be a problem since we have been a customer for at least five years. Ask him to acknowledge receipt of the telegram, and I will want to see that, too." She knew that reluctance to delegate authority was one of her major failings as a manager, and she was working on that. That effort was on hold, however, where Britton was concerned.

"You didn't say who the customer is."

"His name is printed on one of the sheets. Some call him the Prince of Santa Fe. Charles Hanover is the legal name he goes by here."

"Are you suggesting he might be known by other names?"

"Not really, but that is one of the reasons we are making the inquiry. I want Pinkertons to be aware of that possibility."

"Mister Hanover already has an account here."

"I am aware of that, but it seems to be a token account with only occasional deposits and drafts. We welcome any business, but there is a possibility he will be requesting substantial loans."

"I'm not aware that you make this inquiry regarding every customer."

"We don't. Now, I would appreciate it if you would take care of this. You have ample time, so I assume this little project will not interfere with your other work."

"No, ma'am. I will try to have it completed tomorrow, if possible, certainly by the next day."

"Thank you."

Rylee watched Tabor Britton walk back to his workstation. He had seemed more than casually interested in the fact that the subject of her concern was Charles Hanover, but she supposed that was because of her possibly unfair bias toward the young banker. She shrugged off her suspicion. She was glad it was near the end of the workday. She was to have an early dinner at the Exchange Hotel tonight with her longtime beau, Gabriel Laurent, after which they would spend the night together at the

Rivers home which she had to herself for at least three days. Yes, she was ready to rendezvous with Gabe. It had been too long.

Chapter 7

RYLEE TENDED TO the half dozen stabled horses while she awaited Gabe's arrival. They had dined at the Exchange Hotel immediately following work at their respective jobs. Gabe had recently passed the bar examination and moved from his clerkship role at the Rivers & Sinclair law firm to its most junior lawyer.

The pair had been a couple for several years now, and most of their friends and business associates assumed they would marry. Gabe was more than ready. He proposed marriage at least every other month, but she was not ready. She was a decisive woman when it came to business matters, not so much so when it came to some things in her personal life.

She could see herself married to Gabe. Aside from Jael Rivers, one of the law firm's partners, Gabe was her best friend and a patient and wonderful lover. He was unfailingly kind, sometimes too much so. Her temper was quicker, and if she became annoyed or impatient about something, she occasionally snapped a profanity or might direct something hurtful at him. It was all water off a duck's back to him. It especially miffed her when his sole response was a smile. She had never heard him cuss.

His calm, quiet demeanor could not be from his up-bringing, unless his mother had trained him to be an obedient pup. She had never met Gabe's mother but had heard the stories about Lilith La Croix, who was a native of New Orleans where Gabe was raised. She had followed her husband, not coincidentally named Adam, to the Santa Fe area where he had escaped with Gabe's sister to protect his young daughter from the wrath and cruelty of the mother. Lilith, who claimed descent from the presumably mythical Lilith believed by some to be the Biblical Adam's first wife, had murdered the estranged husband, eluded the law, and returned to New Orleans. Gabe did not like to talk about her, but she knew the crazy woman still haunted him, and she wondered if he could be truly happy until that loose end in his life was some-how tied up.

She finished the chores, thankful that the other dozen or so critters had been turned out on the grass. She gen-erally handled livestock care when Jael, Josh, and their fourteen-year-old son Michael were all absent from the place, and she enjoyed it for the most part, glad that she could perform some labor to pay rent that they would not otherwise accept.

Josh's sister, Tabitha, lived in a new home on the adjacent 500-acre tract with her husband Oliver Wolf, a half-blood Cherokee, and their small child. Oliver was a successful artist, and Tabitha had written several best-selling novels, including the acclaimed The Last Hunt. They were always available to help if needed.

She headed for the house and stepped onto the veranda that spanned the frontage of the adobe house just as Gabriel arrived, mounted on his red roan gelding. She had hoped to slip out of her boots and faded blue jeans and change into something more alluring before he appeared. Of course, he was not wearing his business suit tonight.

She stepped out to meet him. "If you're still planning to stay the night, go ahead and stable Sleepy. I'm going to have a glass of wine tonight. I assume you prefer tea."

"Yep. Tea would be nice."

Gabriel was a teetotaler. He abstained from alcohol. This was fine with her. Occasional wine was her only indulgence in the spirits, but it bothered her some that she had been unable to uncover some vice in this young man who was not more than a year older than her. Unless she would be considered a vice.

She abandoned her notion of changing, deciding it was a waste of time since they would likely both be naked within an hour. Just the thought sent a tingle down her spine and a few other places. Gabe was her vice. She was addicted to their intimate moments together and could not imagine a better lover although she had no other experience to draw on. Gabe was a man of limited experience also, and they had fun learning together. They found themselves laughing at some of the silliness they tried.

She slipped off her boots, started heating water on the cookstove for tea, and found a bottle of red wine that she and Jael shared from time to time. She stepped in front of the parlor mirror and retied the ribbon that bound the ponytail in her long sable hair. She had lightly bronzed skin and dark brown eyes from her mother's Spanish heritage, and her Latin characteristics helped her form a bridge to Mexican customers at the bank.

Rylee turned from the mirror when Gabe came through the door. He paused a moment and just looked at her and smiled. Like her, he was dark, descended from a hodgepodge of New Orleans cultures. He stood an inch or two short of six feet, just a bit taller than she. His work suggested he might have soft flesh under his clothing, but she had learned that was far from the truth. He did not carry an ounce of fat, and his body was sheathed with muscle. She had no basis for comparison, but she imagined he would rank high on a list of well-endowed males. She chided herself for a filthy mind and tried to force herself not to think about it.

Gabe stepped toward her with open arms and embraced her tightly. They shared a lingering kiss. Her blood raced, and she swore her heart hammered in her chest. She preferred to be in control of her every action. With Gabe she was not and usually was forced to will herself to take charge of her emotions and rein in her reactions.

"I have tea brewing," Rylee said.

"I would enjoy that later. Do you suppose you could set it aside for a bit?"

"Yes, I guess I could do that." She would gladly do that. They could talk later. They had not been together for almost ten days.

"Can I help with anything?" He followed her through the dining room and into the kitchen.

"I guess you could add a little coal to the cookstove. I assume you purchased condoms?"

"I went to Mystery Manor yesterday evening. Rita has a separate entrance now, so you don't have to enter the bordello to buy merchandise. She has a little shop set up just inside the door. It has some merchandise I'm not brave enough to ask about—not yet anyhow. Rita is an enterprising person, I tell you. She has found ways to get past the Comstock Law."

The Comstock Law was an act of Congress passed some ten years earlier that banned people from sending condoms and other contraceptives and other "immoral goods" through the mail. This was evaded by simply calling contents "gentlemen's goods" or using some other euphemism. There were also many private carriers who would deliver the merchandise with other goods.

She took his hand and led him to the bedroom. "I hope you got the rubber condoms. I'm not fond of the sheep intestines." She giggled. "It was kind of fun tying the ribbon around the base of your pizzle to hold them on, though."

"For you, maybe. Not for me. You tied the darn things too tight."

"After one pulled off that time, I wasn't taking any chances."

Before the mid-1800s, condoms were made from animal intestines—usually those of sheep, calves or goats, resulting often in loose-fitting protection. They were often difficult for the average person to obtain because of excessive costs.

She knew that Gabe and presumably most men were not fond of condoms, but she was taking no more chances than necessary. She was not ready for a child at this time in her career, and marriage was not yet on her calendar either. Fortunately, they were both uninhibited with each other and were adding other options to their menu.

Their first coupling was almost businesslike. They shed their garments quickly, crawled in bed and achieved mutual satisfaction without serious preliminaries. Afterward, they lay naked, Rylee spooned up against Gabe's back with her arm tossed over his chest.

"Are you still planning to stay the night?" Rylee asked.

"Yep. I will get up early so I can get home before sunrise. I don't like for neighbors to see me getting home after sunrise."

"Old Missus Ketchum will likely have her spyglass set on your place all night anyway."

"I suppose. Do you want me out tomorrow night?"

"If you like. As you know, Jael is at the Comanche reservation near Fort Sill meeting with Quanah Parker about some legal matters and won't return for at least a week. Michael is up north at his grandfather's ranch for a few weeks. You could stay the next night, too. I'll fix supper tomorrow night. Next night you can take me to La Castillo's. I'm not cooking more than once, and don't expect anything fancy."

"Josh will be back from Albuquerque after that, I guess. I know he had a meeting with some folks about a land grant problem there. Danna Sinclair usually handles land grant work, but she has a trial over another contested property in the District Court. It just started, and she thinks it could take a week. She wants me in court with her tomorrow."

"Then you need your sleep."

"I don't think so. There's not a chance when I'm here with a naked lady snuggled up against me. I'm not leaving unless you boot me out."

"Just any naked lady?"

"I'm asserting my constitutional right to remain silent."

She slapped him on the butt and rolled away, swinging her long legs off the bed. "Time for tea and wine."

"We can bypass that as far as I'm concerned."

She went to her closet and snatched a long cotton robe. "Not as far as I'm concerned. You are going to have to seduce me back to the bed after I have my wine. I don't care what you do about your tea."

"I can seduce you. I know I can. It's not that difficult."
He got out of bed and picked up his undershorts, facing
her as he slowly pulled them up his legs and thighs.

Rylee sighed and headed for the kitchen. She needed
that glass of wine, maybe two. She was already seduced,
and he knew it, damn him.

Chapter 8

THE PRINCE WAS sitting in his study staring at the wall when Paddy O'Meara interrupted his planning for Miss Jessica Chandler's future.

"We've got company, Boss."

"I don't want to see anybody. You know that."

"It's the bank contact. His name's Tabor Britton."

"You take his message."

"He won't talk to nobody but you. He says you will want the information he's got. I'm guessing he's got more money in mind."

"They always do, these stool pigeons. Well, I want to know what's going on at that bank. I smell trouble with that O'Brian woman."

"She's Irish, Boss. She can't be all bad."

"Maybe so, but she looks more Mexican. These idiots in the west aren't worth a damn at keeping pure bloodlines. They're a bunch of mongrels, or soon will be. I've even seen whites pairing up with coloreds for God's sake. Turns my stomach."

"What about Britton, Boss? He's outside the gate. I've got him perched on the bench out there."

"Let him wait a half hour. Then bring him in."

When O'Meara escorted Britton into the office, Hanover remained seated with his feet propped on the desk, a smoldering cigar lodged in one corner of his mouth. He gave the young man a wave, signaling he should sit down. He looked up at Paddy. "You checked him for weapons?"

"Nothing. He's clean."

"Wait outside the door. When we're finished, I'll holler."

O'Meara nodded and stepped out of the room, closing the door behind him. Britton fidgeted in his chair, waiting for Hanover to speak. The prince leaned forward and snuffed out the cigar on a clayware ashtray. He swung his feet off the desk and straightened in his chair fixing his eyes on the obviously nervous visitor. "So you're our man at the bank? I don't recall seeing you there."

"I guess I wasn't out front the times you have been in, sir. I often work on books in the back room."

"So you're a bookkeeper. I can see that you might have useful information. What was so important you had to see me about it?"

"I do other things besides books. I was hired to be trained to become a loan officer. I am supposed to learn all phases of the bank process first. I'm good with numbers, though, and bookkeeping is where they need the most help now."

"I see, but you have not answered my question. Why did you insist upon seeing me?"

"I have information that could be vital to you, more valuable than what I have been passing along up till now."

"You are wanting more money, aren't you?"

"The first vice-president does not like me. She will see me dismissed if I drag my feet on the task I've been assigned, and I am guessing you would want me to do just that."

"And the first vice-president is Rylee O'Brian."

"Yes, and she is one tough bitch."

"I've met Miss O'Brian. Let's say I am wary of her."

"As well you should be."

"Tell me your story."

"I am selling the story."

"I don't know what I am buying."

"You will have to trust me. I want one thousand dollars."

"I will decide what it's worth. One thousand dollars is an absurd price for any information you might have. I will pay you something if the information is worth anything. And I will let you live."

Britton froze and paled. "What are you saying?"

"If you don't tell me what you came here to sell, you will not show up to work at the bank tomorrow. Let's say you will just disappear."

"Well, I...I always intended to tell you."

"Then do it. I'm a busy man."

"Miss O'Brian has ordered me to make arrangements to have you investigated by the Pinkerton Detective Agency." He told Hanover about Rylee's instructions.

"She spoke to you yesterday afternoon, so that means you must produce a letter by tomorrow morning."

"I have prepared it. I just have not presented it to her."

"After she reviews it, will she allow you to mail the letter?"

"I thought I would offer. It's not the type of detail that a bank officer would usually attend to."

"You will lose that letter but send the telegram alerting Pinkerton as she requested."

"She will learn in a week or ten days."

"By that time, you will not be working there. A bank robbery will occur, and if you cooperate, you will be paid ten per cent of whatever the robbers make off with. Your cooperation will be critical. You come here the next morning and see Paddy, and he will count out your share. We will need each other if this is to succeed, so you deserve to be paid well."

"I am not a gunfighter."

"You will not require a weapon. Tell me, how much cash does the bank generally have on hand?"

"Most of the time, there is a bit under a hundred thousand dollars. It so happens, there is about seven thousand over that right now, nearly fifty thousand in gold coins, mostly the twenty-dollar double eagles. The gold remains in the safe unless a customer demands withdrawal in gold."

"How much of this money is in the clerks' counter drawers?"

"No more than fifteen thousand dollars. Most of the money is kept in the safe and only taken out when needed."

"Is the safe locked during the day?"

"Yes and opened only if needed."

"Who has the combination?"

"Only the president, Mister Spiegelberg and our friend Rylee O'Brian. I suppose the combination is also kept by one of the Spiegelberg brothers at the mercantile center."

"Is there a chance you could find the combination?"

"Almost impossible. It appears to be in their heads. It's not like it is secreted in a desk drawer or anything as near as I know."

"Very well. I will ponder the matter of the safe."

"You should know that O'Brian is just like a daughter to Spiegelberg. He is a widower with no children. I think he would do anything to protect her."

"Hmm. Mister Britton, perhaps you are worth what we will be paying you." He stood. "I will be making some arrangements."

"When is this going to take place?"

"Within a week. You will know when it happens. Get word to me in the meantime if there is anything I should know."

"You won't kill anyone or anything?"

"The folks who will be doing this are bank robbers, not killers—so long as there is cooperation." He walked around the desk and offered his hand to the visitor. "I thank you, Mister Britton. I look forward to a successful partnership."

Britton accepted his hand, offering a grip that might have been that of a dead man's. "Yes, sir."

After Paddy O'Meara escorted Britton out the castle gate where his mount was hitched, he returned to Hanover's office and sat down in front of the desk. It annoyed Hanover that the man never asked if he might sit down or waited for an invitation, but he had learned not to expect respect from the man. He had mostly resigned himself to the man's insolence because he had no choice. O'Meara knew too much, and he required a man with his background to make things happen. Besides, the former Army sergeant handled all the direct contacts with the uncouth and unsavory men who carried out his bidding.

O'Meara said, "The young man seemed happy enough when he left."

"Ignorant fool. His information was helpful, but I didn't part with any cash. He agreed to accept a share of profits from our next project. There will soon be a robbery at the Second National Bank."

"Then you will be wanting me to contact Hackler."

"Yes. As soon as possible. His gang is still holed up at the old cliff dwellings, I assume."

"Yeah, that's a long three days' ride from here, but you're lucky. Tomorrow's the day one of his men will check in with me, likely midafternoon. Hackler's probably getting hungry for some work. He's threatened to take off on his own if we ain't going to give him more to do. He don't like sharing his take on these jobs anyhow."

"We give him better jobs than he would find for himself. We lay the groundwork for him. He does okay."

"He knows that, or he wouldn't be staying on."

"This will be a big one, as much as a hundred thousand at the bank. And I've got a side job I'll pay him extra for."

"Yeah?"

"He is to abduct that crazy female that operates the theater, Jessica Chandler. She's not to return to Santa Fe alive. Same is true for that bank vice-president Rylee O'Brian. And then there is our friend and business partner Tabor Britton. He will be a casualty of the robbery."

"That's a lot of killing, Boss, and killing women won't set well with folks, maybe bring a lot of lawmen here."

"The women are to disappear. I don't want the bodies ever found. That should be easy enough up in those mountains over a hundred miles from here."

"You got eight or nine horny gunslingers up in the Sangre de Cristos that will be wanting to get acquainted with them ladies."

"I don't care. Once they get them to the cliff dwellings, they can have their pleasure for a few days. I don't want the Chandler woman held long, no more than two or three days. The O'Brian bitch, they will hold till I give the word just in case she's needed as a hostage."

"You'd let somebody ransom her?"

"It likely won't work that way, but I've been led to believe she has value to the bank president, and we should possibly hold onto that card for a bit. Eventually, though, she must disappear. We'll have time to ponder this before Hackler and his gang arrive. Tell the messenger they should set up camp at the usual spot out by Jicarilla Creek. Then Hackler can ride in here for instructions."

"This sounds like a complicated job, Boss. Hackler don't know enough to spit downwind, and most of his crew is even dumber."

"We'll keep the instructions simple. You and a few of the boys from here may need to ride up to the cliff dwellings later to make the money split and settle up."

"I still don't see why you're taking the women. That's risky business."

"The Chandler woman is personal. O'Brian is planning to contact Pinkertons to investigate me. There are a few things that happened in Illinois and Indiana that could cause trouble, possibly affect my plans to establish a permanent place here."

"If she talked to her boss about what she's doing, you might just be delaying those problems."

"I sense that she was doing this on her own. Anyway, that's not your concern. You get paid damn well to carry out my instructions."

O'Meara just glared back at him. Sometimes he was not certain he knew anyone he could trust.

Chapter 9

JESSICA CHANDLER WAS miffed. Somebody was pounding on the theater's front door. Couldn't the idiot read the 'closed' sign in the front window? It was not yet noon, and she was not in a mood to deal with people. Lydia Thompson and her British Blondes troupe would arrive tomorrow, and the day after that their burlesque performance would open.

Thankfully, her friend Tabitha Rivers Wolf volunteered to help her with the project and had been helping set up and decorate the stage the past week. Tabby, a former newspaper reporter, was a well-known author of two best-selling books, The Last Hunt, a historical fiction novel of Quanah's surrender and leading his Comanche band to the reservation, and Dismal Trail, a non-fiction work about her experience as a newspaper correspondent during the last days of the Comanche wars.

Tabby would have entered through the back door and wasn't due for an hour yet. While she had known Tabby, her lawyer's younger sister, for some years, they had only recently forged a friendship, and she planned to tell the younger woman today about her pregnancy. She had endured trials of her own, including life as a captive of the Apache war chief, El Gato, and she was the mother of a little girl not yet three years old. Tabby was wise beyond her years and not inclined to be judgmental.

She pulled the curtain back and peered out the window and saw a buckboard behind two mules in the big lot fringed by hitching rails originally installed to accommodate the congregation when a Catholic church formerly occupied the structure. A large wooden box the size of a coffin sat in the wagon bed. The angle allowed her to see just part of a tall man standing at the theater door. He wore a coat and appeared respectably attired.

She walked over to the door and released the bolt lock on the heavy, ornately carved double doors and pulled one door partly open. It sprang back and slammed her head, sending her reeling backwards till she collapsed on the terra cotta tile floor. She was dazed when a mustachioed man with reptilian eyes dropped to his knees and handcuffed her. She was vaguely aware of someone else cinching her ankles together with rope before a cloth gag came over her mouth and was knotted behind her upper neck.

Her attackers disappeared, and she fought against her bonds, rolling on the floor seeking something that might help loosen the ankle bindings, but her efforts were futile. She was near panic now, because she had always suffered an irrational fear of imposed immobility and confinement.

Then the man returned with a shorter, stockier man who must have been helping him. They carried the wooden box and sat it down beside her. Oh, my God. They were going to put her in that thing. She would rather die. She began to scream, but the sound was muffled by her gag. She fought and struggled when the tall man slipped his hand under her arms and the other grabbed her legs, and they slung her into the box. If only they would just shoot her. What was this all about? It made no sense.

The invaders had not uttered a word. Their visit had been well thought out. When the lid came over the box and launched her into pitch-blackness, she closed her eyes and prayed for death to claim her.

Chapter 10

RYLEE OCCASIONALLY MET Gabe for lunch, but this morning he was again appearing with Danna Sinclair in the territorial court on a Spanish land grant case. He thought he was being groomed to take on such cases, since they were becoming an increasing priority for the Rivers & Sinclair firm and were generally quite lucrative. He had told Rylee that he didn't mind. He knew some lawyers would find the work boring, but he enjoyed the historical research and just wanted to carve a niche for himself in the firm. He loved his co-workers and the challenges offered by the law.

She was pleased by his attitude, partially because she thought of Josh and Jael Rivers—and Michael, of course—as her family, but, also, because she was seeking a life that offered some stability. Gabe was still pressing her to marry him, and their successive nights at the Rivers' house had given her new incentive. Ordinarily, their intimacy was confined to her occasional nocturnal visits to his two-room adobe house and, weather permitting, a Sunday afternoon visit to one of several love nests they had claimed in the surrounding countryside.

Rylee was tired of sneaking around like a criminal to rendezvous with her lover and was very close to accepting his proposal and establishing a home with this man. Above the monthly payments she made for food-cost sharing to Jael and Josh, which she insisted upon paying, she had saved most of her earnings from the bank since her employment. Gabe assured her that he had nearly five thousand dollars in gold coins stashed someplace. They could easily buy a modest home that would give them at least a few more rooms without exhausting all their funds. She would never let money leave her hand casually, and she conceded to being beyond frugal. Perhaps they would have a serious discussion soon.

She decided to forget lunch for now. Willi Spiegelberg was attending a family business meeting with his brothers and was not due back till two o'clock or later, and she felt she should be available to staff and customers.

She turned back to the loan files on her desk and was absorbed with review of the paperwork documenting a usually reliable customer's delinquent loan when she heard a disturbance in the bank's public area. She looked up, and through the window saw five hooded men swinging pistols toward customers and employees. She slid her desk drawer open and removed her own loaded Smith & Wesson before thinking better of it and returning the weapon to its resting place. For the safety of customers and employees, she did not want to start gunplay.

Her mind raced. The safe was locked. The bank could survive the loss of money in the cash drawers out front. It was best not to resist and hope the law would catch up with these thieves. She decided to go out and instruct employees to cooperate.

By the time she stepped out of her office doorway, it appeared the tellers were already emptying the cash drawers into denim bags furnished by the robbers. A thin hooded man was already headed her way with his pistol pointed at her midsection. She stopped and waited.

In a surprisingly shrill voice, he said, "You the vice-president lady?"

"I am."

"Where's the president? I want to talk with him."

"That would be Willi Spiegelberg. He is not in the bank today."

"We want in the safe."

"It's locked. You cannot enter it."

"You know the combination. Don't deny it. We got that on good authority."

She said nothing, and just stared at him. She was scared, but they would not get into the vault on her watch.

"Answer me, bitch."

At that moment, she saw Tabor Britton standing at his desk watching her with a smirk on his face. He was in on this, of course. That made her even more determined.

The robber stepped up to her and pressed his gun to her temple. "You got two choices, sweets. Open the vault. Or die."

"You are a fool if you kill me or anybody else. You will have the law and the United States Army on your trail."

"I will count to three. Then I squeeze the trigger."

A sturdy man with a limp approached. "Drawers are cleaned out, chief, and the boys are searching the customers now."

"This bitch is about to give me the safe combination."

At least her death should be quick, Rylee figured. She was not going to surrender the combination.

The outlaw said, "One...two...three."

She bit her lower lip, steeling herself for the end.

Instead, the gun barrel smashed against her head, nearly knocking her off her feet. Blood trickled down her forehead and dripped over her right eye. The man grabbed her arm and nearly yanked her off her feet as he passed her to the other outlaw.

"This is our hostage. Take her out to the spare horse and get her in the saddle." He yelled, "You folks all stay put in the bank till you can't see nothing but our dust or this lady dies. If that happens, we'll come back and feed you a bit of lead."

Rylee looked back as the outlaw half drug her toward the door. She was aghast when she saw the man called 'boss' raise his pistol and the weapon thundered twice, driving two slugs into Tabor Britton's chest. Then he backed out of the building, his gun swinging and inviting anyone to challenge him.

After that, Rylee rode away, her hands gripping the saddle horn while one of the robbers led her mount. Gunfire midday was not all that uncommon in Santa Fe. Except for those people in the bank and a few who saw the robbers exit, most would have no more than a bit of curiosity. She had no illusions. Her adventure would not be over quickly, and her death sentence may only have been delayed.

Chapter 11

GABRIEL LAURENT WALKED out of the Federal Courthouse, briefcase in hand, beside Danna Sinclair, one of the law firm's name partners. A tall, willowy strawberry-blonde woman with sapphire blue eyes and Nordic features, Danna was the office's managing partner, Josh Rivers having little interest in attending to the business side of the firm. No more than a year or two past thirty, Danna had acquired a reputation in the legal community as the last word on land grant law.

Danna pointed toward the Second National Bank building some two blocks distant. "There's a near mob gathered outside the bank, folks running back and forth. Those gunshots we heard during closing argument...you don't suppose?"

"I've got to find out," Gabe said. "Do you mind if I take a detour?"

"Rylee. Of course, you are concerned. Go right ahead. Just bring some news with you when you come back to the office."

Gabe headed down the boardwalk at a trot. When he reached the bank, he made his way through the crowd, rightly figuring the onlookers would yield to a man wearing a suit and carrying a briefcase. He just needed to make it appear that he had a mission there. He did: confirming that Rylee was unharmed.

His heart raced when he entered the bank, and he could not see her anyplace. Willi Spiegelberg, flushed and visibly shaken, stood in front of Rylee's office speaking with United States Marshal Chance Calder and a taller, thin, suited man wearing a sombrero. Both the balding, gray-haired banker and marshal stood no more than five and a half feet tall, so with the sombrero, the stranger probably seemed taller than his actual height.

As he approached, the men turned his way, and the banker said something to the stranger, probably explaining Gabe's presence. Spiegelberg stepped a few paces away from the other two and to welcome him.

"Gabriel, I am glad you are here, young friend. They have taken our Rylee." The banker spoke perfect English but with a trace of German accent. The only Jewish family in Santa Fe, the Spiegelberg parents had immigrated to

America before the five boys and only sister were born, but German had still been the children's first language.

"What do you mean? Who has taken her? Why?"

"Bank robbers." Spiegelberg nodded toward a cluster of bank employees gathered behind the cashiers' counter and Doctor Micah Rand, who had just got to his feet and looked their way, shaking his head from side to side. "I wasn't here, but they said poor Tabor Britton was shot down in cold blood. He was not resisting or doing anything to incite the shooter."

Gabe could see Britton's legs now sticking out from behind his desk and a pool of blood on the floor. "But why did they take Rylee?"

"She is apparently a hostage to assure that the law doesn't chase them down. And she refused to open the vault or provide the combination, one of the tellers told me. I am hoping they demand a ransom, so we can recover her without violence. She is...is very special. I cannot imagine a demand I would not pay." He patted Gabe on the shoulder. "Come join us. You know Marshal Calder, of course. The other gentleman is a deputy U.S. marshal in town on special assignment."

Gabe liked and trusted Calder, a Georgia native who had fought for the Confederacy. Following the war, he served the blue and was a top sergeant under Colonel

Ranald Mackenzie during the Comanche wars. A fifty-ish man, wiry with salt and pepper mustache and long, neatly trimmed sideburns, his deep southern accent took Gabe back to his Louisiana roots.

"Afternoon, Gabe." Marshal Chase Calder said when he joined the men. "This here is Deputy U.S Marshal Brigham Paris."

Paris extended his hand, and Gabe returned a firm grip. "'Brig will do."

Calder said, "Gabe's one of our local law wranglers. He also happens to be Miss O'Brian's fiancée."

"Then I guess you're entitled to know what's going on. We're digging into deep shit here, my friend."

"Why aren't we getting a posse together to go after these men? I'll be ready to ride in twenty minutes."

Paris fingered one side of a black, handlebar mustache that looked like a pair of steer horns protruding from beneath his nose across his pale, skeletal face. "This ain't the time to push these devils. They already got their head start. If we crowd these kind of men with an army, I'm afraid the young lady don't have much chance. My guess is they haven't decided what to do with her yet, but they're likely thinking she's worth some ransom."

Gabe said, "We can't sit here and wait a week for a ransom message to come."

"Nope. But they'll be waiting for instructions from somebody. I'm sure of it. My guess is that person can't resist the possibility of milking more cash out of this bank. A message will come, but we ain't waiting for it."

Spiegelberg said, "We will pay the ransom, whatever it is."

"The ransom is just buying us time," Paris said. "They won't turn the young lady loose alive."

Paris seemed certain of his prediction, and it sent a wave of weakness through Gabe's body. "Then what are you proposing to do, marshal? You sound like you know more about these men than you are telling us."

"I'm not free to say just yet. But I'm in Santa Fe because I've been trying to rope the mastermind of this bunch for over two years now. He's got four, maybe five, outfits that hold up banks, trains or anyplace where there's money. My job is to put this fella out of business, maybe see him hang. And what do I propose to do? I want three or four men to ride with me, so we can move more quiet-like than a big posse. A tracker would be good."

"Count me in."

"Son, we need men of a different sort than those that carry on their fights in a courtroom."

"I can ride with the best, and I grew up in New Orleans. I'm no stranger to guns—or knives for that matter.

I'll be carrying both. I'm not going to sit here on my ass and wait for somebody to report what's going on."

Paris sighed. "I guess you're signed on."

Gabe said, "I'm certain you are going to have another lawyer riding with you, too."

"No, that won't do."

"One of my bosses, Josh Rivers, is sort of a foster parent to Rylee. He's fought Comanches, trailed them for years looking for his abducted son. You won't say no to Josh. And he grew up on a ranch at the base of the Sangre de Cristo mountains some miles north of here. He knows this country. His wife is at Fort Sill right now, or you'd be taking her, too."

"Can he track?"

"Some, I think. But you'll be wanting Oliver Wolf for that."

"You just got this all figured out, don't you, young man?"

Marshal Calder interceded. "Wolf is your man if he'll do it. He's heavy on Cherokee blood, and he's taken on jobs as a special deputy to me more times than I can count. He scouted for the Army during the Red River War against the Comanche and Kiowa. I worked with him then. Let me talk to him. I'll deputize him if you like, so you'll have another lawman with your bunch."

Paris said, "If you recommend this Wolf, that's good enough for me. I assume you'll stay in town to deal with any ransom messages that come in."

"Yep. I've got a gimpy back that can't handle the kind of saddle time you'll be putting in anyhow. I'm not sure how they'd get a message to us if they're on the run."

"The message will come from a man in Santa Fe but not direct, of course."

"You're saying they've got somebody here in town involved?"

"The man I've been asking questions about. Charles Hanover, the pompous ass who styles himself the Prince of Santa Fe. I don't have the evidence to take him down yet, but I'm betting he's the head of this operation."

"When do we leave?" Gabe asked. "I'll run over to the office and tell Josh. He just got back last night from handling a case in Albuquerque."

"Meet at 'The Stable.' We ride out at sunrise."

"Sunrise? I thought we'd leave this afternoon. We'll be giving them a day's head start."

"They won't be riding all night. Men and horses will need rest. I'll be arranging for food and gear and a pack-horse this afternoon. Just bring any personals you need."

Calder said. "We won't have any way to contact you if a ransom message comes in."

"You just play that out as best you can. They ain't going to turn that young woman over once she sees their faces. She's dead if we don't get her back before they decide she's not useful anymore."

The cold words angered Gabe, yet he understood the deputy was stating a harsh truth. He realized also that the delay till morning made sense. Marshal Calder needed to contact Oliver Wolf, and Josh Rivers had not been informed yet that he had volunteered for the mission. But he did not like it, and nothing had happened to reduce his angst for Rylee's well-being.

Chapter 12

JOSH RIVERS PACED around the conference room table, waiting for Gabe to return to the office. Danna had told him about a disturbance near the bank his young associate had gone to investigate, but she had not appeared especially concerned about it. A short time later, Linda de la Cruz entered his office to report that Rylee had been taken hostage by bank robbers and that a bank employee, whose name he did not recognize, was shot and killed.

He was beyond worried about Rylee, and when he knew more, he would send a telegram to Jael at Fort Sill. She would likely make train connections and head home. If he delayed telling her, there would be hell to pay when she found out. She and Jael were like sisters most times, mother and daughter at others. He felt fatherly when it came to Rylee, although he was no more than fifteen or so years older. Regardless, she was family, and she seemed to reciprocate those feelings, having watched her parents die at the hands of Comancheros as a thirteen-year-old. She had been spared as prospective merchandise at a Mexican bordello.

He plucked his watch from his vest pocket. It had been an hour since Danna returned to the office. If Gabe didn't show up in ten minutes, he decided he would head for the bank and find out himself what the blazes was going on.

When Gabe's time was up, he headed for the office door. He stopped at Linda de la Cruz's desk behind the counter that separated her from the client waiting area. "Linda, if Gabe shows up, tell him to stay put till I return, I've got to find out what's happening at the bank, and what the law is going to do."

"I will hogtie him if I must."

He reached for the door handle and was almost knocked off his feet when the door pushed back at him, and his sister Tabby burst through. "Oh, sorry, Josh," Tabby said. "Glad I caught you. You are the person I'm here to see."

"I'm in a hurry, Tab."

She rolled the cocoa-brown eyes that appeared just below the wide-brimmed Plainsman hat that was tugged down on her forehead. With her closely shorn chestnut hair and doeskin shirt and britches and moccasins, first glance might suggest she was a half-blood Indian boy. Second glance, however, would reveal a beautiful lithe young woman with smooth, olive skin and gentle curves in the right places.

"You're always in a dang hurry, but you're going to hear me out."

He sighed. "Let's step into my office, little sis."

She followed him out of the waiting room and down the hallway to his office. Tabitha Rivers was accustomed to getting her way with four older brothers. She was almost seven years younger than Josh, having just turned thirty, and the product of an adulterous relationship between her father, Levi Rivers, and a half-blood Navajo woman some twenty-five years younger. The mother, named Summer, died during childbirth and Levi's wife, Aurelie, had taken her in to raise with the four boys. Tabby, Cal, and Josh had been unaware of her patchwork ancestry until five or six years earlier. The other older brothers, Nathan and Hamilton, had assumed she was adopted and never gave it much thought. There was no time for curiosity about such things at the Slash R Ranch.

Josh did not sit down in his office or offer his sister a chair. He did not want to encourage a long conversation. "Okay, spill it out."

"You've heard about the bank robbery and Rylee?"

"Yes, but not enough. I was just heading to the bank to see if I can find out more. Gabe Laurent's supposed to be there but should have reported in by now. I've got to find out what I can do, maybe join a posse if there is one. Head out on my own otherwise."

"Well, add this to your plate. Jessica's disappeared."

"Disappeared. What do you mean?"

"That education at Hastings Law College in California was sure a waste if you don't know what disappeared means. She can't be found anyplace, and that's not Jessica. I was supposed to meet her at the theater this morning to help prepare for the burlesque show that's coming in. She always leaves a note on her office desk if she stepped out someplace. She did not. I went to her hotel suite. She wasn't there. The desk clerk said she left at eight o'clock this morning, and he was sure she hadn't been back. When she didn't answer to my knocking, the clerk did open the door and let me take a quick look."

"She could be a lot of places. Jessica's probably just out shopping and lost track of time and forgot you were coming."

"No. She doesn't do that, and with a show coming in, she has too much to do. And there's something else."

"Yeah? Spit it out."

"I talked to some of the neighbors. The theater is set back a good distance from the road, but Hank at the barbershop only two buildings north on the opposite side saw two men pull up at the theater in a wagon this morning. They had a big coffin-like crate in the wagon bed and carried it up to the building. He couldn't tell if they took the crate inside, but it was a good half hour before the men returned to the wagon with that crate and drove off."

"And you are thinking Jessica was in that crate."

"Yes."

He would not argue with her on that suspicion. "He didn't recognize the men?"

"Strangers, he said, one a big man. The other not so much. The big man had a bristly black mustache that needed a barber's trim. Both could use haircuts. Anglos. He couldn't tell me much else that would make them any different from most Anglo ranch hands in these parts."

Suddenly, he heard Gabe's distinctive New Orleans voice in the outer office. "Go ahead and sit down, Tabby. I'll hustle Gabe in here." He went to the open doorway and hollered, "Gabe. Come to my office as soon as you can."

Momentarily, Gabe appeared. "Linda says you've heard what happened at the bank."

"Yeah, now sit down and tell me and Tabby what's being done about it."

Gabe let himself down in the chair next to Tabby, and Josh took his own behind the desk. For the next twenty minutes, Gabe laid out his conversation at the bank with Spiegelberg, U.S. Marshal Calder, and Brigham Paris, the deputy U.S. marshal.

Josh said, "And this Paris is here investigating Charles Hanover?"

"Like I said, he suspects Hanover is the mastermind behind a lot of bank and train robberies, mostly west of the Mississippi. They've just never been able to get the evidence to lead directly to him. He apparently avoids direct contact with those who do jobs. Men have gone to the gallows not knowing who had hired them."

"And Paris wants me to ride with him?"

"Yeah, and Oliver Wolf and me. I insisted on going. I don't suppose Danna is going to like both of us being gone, but I've got to do this even if I'm risking my job."

"You aren't risking your job. I'll talk to Danna. She will be more understanding than you might think. She's not as tough as she pretends to be. Besides, Marty Locke is here from the Fort Sill office till Jael returns. Our office folks can juggle things while we're gone. I can't see this taking more than a week, probably less."

Tabby said, "I don't like it that my husband gets in on this, and I don't."

"Somebody's got to take care of Luna."

"I know. But she'd rather be with Oliver. He's more patient than I am. And then, I guess the show must go on as they say. I'll have to see if I can greet the burlesque troupe that's coming in and make the performances happen. It won't help with a two-year-old getting into everything. But I just want Jess and Rylee back safely. I hope they are together, and we're not up against separate abductions."

Gabe said, "No way to know for certain yet, but I'll talk to the marshal or Paris before I head home. They need to know about Jessica's disappearance. We're pulling out at sunrise."

"I assume somebody has asked Oliver about this?"

Gabe said, "Marshall Calder was headed out to your place when I left the bank."

"He's working on a commissioned painting right now, but I can't imagine him saying no. He won't know that I've been told, so when he talks to me about it, I may devil him a bit about abandoning me again. I don't like Oliver or any of you riding into danger, but, yes, you've got to go. My royalties from the other books are drying up, and my publishers are pushing me for another."

Josh chided her. "I'm aware of the prices some of Oliver's works are bringing these days. Don't look for sympathy here."

"I just don't like to be outdone. You know that."

"I know." Tabby, the little sister, had been competing with her older brothers and everyone else she met up with since she was a toddler. She could likely outshoot and certainly outride, any of her male siblings.

Tabby got up. "I'm heading home to talk with that husband of mine. He's going to be leaving me with all the horse chores, so I'm going to see that he cleans the stalls tonight."

Poor Oliver. It was fortunate that he was a calm, stoic man who was not given to either verbal or physical fisti-cuffs. Tabby had tied the knot with a man who was as un-perturbable as any in the territory. Because of that, the marriage just might endure.

Chapter 13

RYLEE HAD BEEN surprised when the bank robbers took her on a wagon path that edged the creek only a few miles north of Santa Fe, and even more puzzled when they came upon a wagon carrying a coffin-sized box. The men had removed their hoods now, obviously abandoning any effort to hide identities. She supposed they also calculated that hooded riders were guaranteed to draw the attention of any observers. It also virtually guaranteed that they did not intend to abandon or return her alive.

The tall, thin shooter at the bank was the obvious leader of the outlaws, all of whom called him "Hack." He was a middle-aged man with a thick, graying mustache and face leathery and dark from many years baking in the sun. He issued orders in a manner suggesting a military background, and she had already tagged Hack as the man she would need to outsmart when she made her attempt to escape. When, not if.

As they rode into the clearing where the wagon sat, Hack hollered, "Tomcat, Jackson, show yourselves."

A few minutes later, a cluster of willows and young cottonwoods parted, and two riders and another saddled, riderless sorrel emerged.

"Where's the woman?" Hack asked.

A round-faced man with a splayed mustache resembling a cat's whiskers above his lips, said. "In the box where you told us to put her." Tomcat was a big, hulking man, and the fleshy face was accentuated by angry, gray eyes that were so light that at first glance they appeared nearly colorless. Hack and Tomcat obviously had no love for each other.

"Well, get her the hell out and onto that horse. You turned the mules loose, so the wagon ain't going no place unless you're planning on doing the pulling."

"You said to put her in the box and bring her here. You didn't say nothing about taking her out."

"Tomcat...never mind...just get her out."

Rylee could not imagine who the poor woman in the box might be or why she might be here.

The two men dismounted. The short, stocky man, Jackson, Rylee assumed, was in the wagon bed by the time Tomcat dismounted and plodded over to the wagon. He easily pried the box lid off and pushed it aside. He reached inside and pulled a woman out and dropped her on the planked wagon bed floor. What she at first thought was a corpse moved.

"Cut her loose and unlock the handcuffs," Hack said.

A few minutes later, with Jackson's help, the woman sat up and tried to take in the scene with squinting eyes, obviously blinded by the sun after being confined to total blackness. Her eye's met with Rylee's, and she froze. Now, Rylee realized that the pale, frazzled woman was Jessica Chandler, a pathetic creature with tangled hair and hollow eyes far unlike the poised, always immaculate, woman she often encountered at the bank and, of course, the theater which was of more interest to Gabe than herself. Jessica's countenance was nothing short of pathetic and she wished she could help her.

But why would Jessica be a captive? It made no sense, especially removing her from town in that box.

Jackson, a man with a black, close-cropped beard and heavy-lidded eyes, grabbed Jessica roughly by her wrist and dragged her to the rear of the wagon and rolled her off into Tomcat's arms. The hefty, clumsy man could not hold her and dropped her on the rocky ground. He pulled her to her feet, gave her a kiss on the lips, and clutched her breast with his free hand.

Hack yelled, "Damn it, Tomcat. Not now. Get that woman on the horse and stop pawing her. We've got to be riding."

Jessica did not resist when they lifted her into the saddle. Poor Jessica, Rylee thought. She rarely rode a horse, and dresses were not made for comfortable riding. Her own thighs and crotch were already hurting without the help of her denim britches and boots she was accustomed to wearing when she rode to work every morning, changing into office wear after arrival at the bank.

Hack said, "You women, we're freeing up your hands to ride. You pull any stunts, and you'll be hogtied and ride belly-down across a horse's back like a dead deer. Do as you're told, and you got a good chance of being set free."

Rylee did not believe that for an instant, but she was not interested in being bound to her horse either. Time was precious, but she guessed she might have a few days' value to these men as a hostage. She was baffled by Jessica's presence, however, and her presence complicated her own escape effort. She could not leave Jessica behind, but she worried about the theater director's ability to survive in the wilderness.

Survival in the forested mountains was the pathway out of this. Afoot, she could go places that these men could not take their horses, and they did not seem the sort who would travel well without sitting on their saddle-toughened asses. She had not the slightest doubt that with a fifty-yard head start, they would never catch her. But with Jessica in tow? Hopefully, she would have an opportunity soon to talk to her fellow captive.

The two women soon got near enough to speak as they rode single file along the creek bank angling northwesterly into the mountains. Three men rode in front led by Hack, and the other four followed behind with the two women in between, Rylee following Jessica.

As suspected, Jessica was not an accomplished rider and shifted frequently in the saddle searching for comfort she never found. Sometimes, Rylee feared Jessica would topple off. She had seen a large purplish knot on the side of the theater director's head indicating a fall or blow, and she supposed that Jessica could be suffering from the injury.

The riders finally broke away from the creek trail, which Rylee figured made good sense if they were being followed, as she assumed was the case. She was surprised when they did not stop at dusk and continued the journey for another hour or more to a clearing in the forest backed by a sheer granite cliff wall on the north and west sides. With its higher ground the site was obviously chosen for its defensibility, and their captors had no doubt camped here before.

She reined in and her arm was immediately clutched by Tomcat who yanked her off her mount and tossed her to the ground before dragging her over shale to the cliff's base and dropping her there. With her skirt hiked above her waist, he had not been able to resist racing his rough fingers up her inner thigh before walking away. The man's brains clearly lay below his belt.

Tomcat ranked high on the list of potential problems. On the other hand, she thought, he didn't know dung from wild honey. She just might be able to turn him into an unwitting accessory to her escape.

Suddenly, Jessica stumbled from the darkness, tumbling half onto Rylee as she fell. The one-eyed man called Patch walked away, apparently having shoved the theater director to the ground. Rylee scooted over, helping Jessica sit up and rest her back against the stone wall. She felt the woman's body shaking, and although she could barely make out her face in the darkness, could hear her sobs.

She wrapped an arm about Jessica's shoulders and pulled her close and spoke just above a whisper. "Jess, you're not in this alone now. We'll find a way out of this."

"I don't want out. I just want to die."

"You don't mean that. You've just been through a lot. You seemed dizzy when we were on the horses, and it looked like you hurt your head. What happened?"

"I'm still light-headed, and it hurts," she said between sobs. "The door. When the men came to the theater for me, one of them forced his way in and slammed the door against my head. I hardly remember what happened after that until they started to put me in that box—the coffin. And then I prayed to die. I have never known such terror, and I will never get over it. This will haunt me to my last breath, and I am ready to end it all."

"Don't talk like that. Things will get better, I promise." She was unsure about the truth of her words, but to say or think otherwise was surrender, and that was not her nature.

She went silent when she saw a shadowy form moving their way. As the shadow drew nearer, she saw it was Hack, the apparent overseer of the bunch.

He dropped a blanket on the ground in front of them. Then he set an open can at Rylee's feet, and working a canteen strap off his shoulder, lay the vessel next to the can. He reached into his pocket, pulled out some strips that Rylee guessed to be jerky, and tossed it on the blanket. "Your supper and morning's breakfast," Hack said.

"Blanket for sleeping. Don't bitch and moan, because we ain't got things any better. We got two days hard riding ahead, so don't waste your rations."

He started to leave and turned back. "Almost forgot. Take off your shoes and give them to me. I don't want you getting any stupid notions you can just get up and walk out of here. And I promise if you try, you are dead. We ain't got time for that foolishness, and you'll be put down quick if you get such ideas."

Rylee figured he could keep the dang shoes if he wanted. Those heeled torturers she wore at the bank would be far worse than barefoot maneuvering through the rocks and undergrowth in mountain country.

The women quickly surrendered their shoes. She was grateful he did not take the long stockings that might be welcome when the night mountain chill set in. After Hack returned to his men, who were setting up camp more than thirty feet distant nearer the trees, Rylee took stock of their position. At least the distance allowed the captives the opportunity to talk privately if they kept their voices soft. Unfortunately, between the campfire and the moonlight, they were afforded no privacy for bodily functions and the women were well illuminated should they attempt to stray too far.

Not that it mattered. Jessica was not ready mentally or physically for an attempted escape, and it was not in Rylee to abandon her involuntary comrade. Riley picked up the can. Beans. No spoon. She offered it to Jessica. "We'll have to drink the beans. You can have first drink."

Jessica grimaced. "I'm not hungry, and I hate beans anyway."

Rylee was a bit miffed. "They didn't give us a menu, and we've got to eat to maintain our strength."

"Help yourself." She waved the can away.

Rylee took her companion at her word and silently drank a third of the can, thinking Jessica would relent later and that they might salvage some for morning. She picked up two jerky strips and again offered one to Jessica, who rejected it with a shake of her head. Rylee sighed. "There are four more. Eat those when you are ready."

"He pulled them from his britches' pocket with his filthy hand. God knows what kind of vermin are growing on them."

Rylee shrugged. "We've got to eat."

"I don't."

Rylee ate the two jerky strips, deciding they were venison and certainly edible. Then she got up and walked ten paces along the cliff wall, figuring that was the limit without triggering a chase. Facing the wall, she lifted up her skirt and pulled down her cotton underpants giving the abductors a look at her ass before she squatted and relieved her aching bladder. When she returned to Jessica's side, she faced the woman's disbelieving stare.

"They were staring at you, every one of them. Are you trying to lure them over here?"

"I had to pee. I held it back for hours. Besides, I doubt a woman's pissing is a terribly seductive act."

"But you did it so casually. I can't do that. I'll wait till everyone is asleep."

"I was a Comanchero captive for weeks. I guess I lost my modesty during that time. I intend to heed nature's call whenever I have the chance. I will certainly sleep better." She snatched up the blanket and pulled it up over their legs. "I am going to grab some shuteye in a moment, but first I need to understand something."

"What is that?" Her voice was a near croak now.

"I was taken hostage during a bank robbery. I may be held for ransom, but it will be money wasted because I will not be allowed to leave alive. If nothing else, I will be shot dead at the time of any exchange. I hope that Willi Spiegelberg has better sense than to fork over even a dollar to these no-goods."

"You don't know that they would kill you."

"I do know, and I intend to escape first. Now, what I need to understand—why are you here?"

"I'm not sure."

"But you have a suspicion?"

"Charles Hanover."

"Hanover? This is beginning to make a little sense."

"What do you mean?"

"I think Hanover is behind the bank robbery."

"You aren't serious?"

"Very serious. And if you have offended him in some way, now that you have seen these men, your life isn't worth any more than mine. You must escape with me."

"How? Where would we go?"

"The forest. Even if we could take horses, this bunch would ride us down in no time. It's slow going horseback out into the woods or moving up or down steep slopes. Horses can't even get through some of that rough country. Men like this can't move once they're forced off their asses. Those boots aren't made for hiking either."

"I would never keep up with you. You're so young and obviously accustomed to a more rugged life. I was raised in St. Louis. I am a town girl."

"Oh, that's nonsense. You're not some old granny."

"But I'm on my way to being a mother."

The statement silenced Rylee. She didn't know what to say and had to think about this and how her plans would be affected.

Jessica continued. "I don't think I am much over two months with child, certainly not a full three months. The father is the prince. Mister Charles Hanover. And I just learned he has a wife and children who will soon join him in Santa Fe. I could be a worry and inconvenience in his mind, although I would never interfere in his life. I would welcome his non-existence, but he cannot imagine someone in my position not resorting to blackmail to profit off his vulnerability."

"I have encountered the man. Yes, I think you are right. He wants you killed at some point. It's possible that his hired guns have been authorized to pleasure themselves with you for a few days first. That is likely in store for both of us when we get to our destination."

Jessica said, "I will go with you, but you must leave me if I cannot keep up. I wish you could obtain a gun and just shoot me if that becomes a problem."

Rylee was not about to tell her about the derringer belted to her right inner thigh with two bullets that she would save for someone special. "We'll be on horseback again tomorrow. We need sleep." She lay back and rolled over onto her side, facing away from her companion and pulling the blanket up over her shoulders.

"Shouldn't we have the blanket under us?" Jessica asked.

"We can't have both. It's going to get dang cold before the night's over. Over is better than under, trust me."

"But the dirt and rocks..."

"You'll get used to it. We're lucky to have a blanket. When it gets cold, we need to snuggle up against each other for body heat. Just do it. I won't take offense, and I hope you won't either."

"I won't be able to sleep."

Ten minutes later, Jessica dropped off to sleep before Rylee did.

Chapter 14

MEMBERS OF THE four-man posse met at "The Stable," a fledgling business owned and operated by Moses "Mose" Monroe, who had previously earned his living as a stableman for the local aristocracy. A few years previous, he had decided to strike out on his own, purchasing an abandoned stable and pens some four blocks east of the Plaza, repairing the decrepit structures and buying a half dozen good horses for rent or trade.

With over twenty stalls, Monroe stabled a good number of horses for the day, and Josh Rivers, confident of the care that Monroe provided, boarded his buckskin gelding "Chief" at The Stable while working in his law office. Brig Paris's big sorrel gelding had been stabled there since the owner's arrival in Santa Fe, and Josh suspected Mose Monroe had furnished the deputy marshal a treasure trove of information during that time. Stablemen knew even more than barbers about the lives of folks in western towns and villages.

Mose, a tall, rail-thin Negro man with deep-set dark eyes stood silently in the alleyway while Paris saddled his mount. Josh stood not far away, and Gabe Laurent and Oliver Wolf waited with the horses in front of the stable. Josh could tell that Mose was waiting to say something. The dark man with snow-white hair and the still raw-looking circle of scar tissue about his neck from a lynching he had survived many years earlier, waited till Paris had the horse saddled and started to lead the horse away and then spoke in his deep, mellifluous voice. "Mister Marshal, I know you've got a more important job right now, but I've got me a worry I'd like to lay on you."

Obviously annoyed, Paris stopped and turned to Mose. "I'm in a rush, Mose, but spit it out."

"Somebody made off with my buckboard and two mules. They was going to rent it for an afternoon, but it ain't showed up. One mule did, though. Ruth walked into the stable late last night, so now I'm missing me just one mule and the wagon."

"You'll have to talk to Marshal Calder about that. I won't have time to be looking for your wagon and mule."

Josh said, "Who rented the wagon, Mose?"

"Never seen them before. One was a tall, solid feller that looked like he could carry a railroad tie in each arm. Scary dang eyes and bristly mustache. He gave his name as John Newton, but I doubt that was his real handle. He called his partner 'Jackson.' He was on the short, stocky side, likely not much hair with his hat off. He didn't do no talking."

Josh said, "Marshal, I think this could be important. I mentioned the other missing woman. There is good reason to believe she was taken from the theater in a box and loaded on a buckboard behind a mule team. I don't think it's a huge jump to think that the same people who took Rylee O'Brian are involved."

"They couldn't be two places at once."

"No. But the gang could have split up."

"That's true. There is another thing. The Chandler woman had been keeping company with the so-called prince, Mister Charles Hanover, who is my top suspect for the bank robbery."

Josh was relieved that Paris was aware of the connections. Jessica had spoken to him with the assurance of lawyer-client confidentiality. There was more to the story than Paris knew, but Jessica's status as an expectant mother was irrelevant at this point. The deputy marshal had accepted the possibility that the two abductions were not likely coincidental.

Paris looked at Mose who was awaiting an answer. "We will be looking for your wagon, Mose, but I don't see much chance we will come across the mule. It seems more likely the critter will find its way here."

"I suppose. Andrew's a contrary animal and don't behave too good. Anybody that's got him now will likely send him on his way. I don't got another decent wagon, so I'd sure welcome it back."

When the pursuers were saddled in front of the stable, Paris looked at Oliver Wolf. "Well, Oliver. I'm told you know this country and have some scouting experience. Where do you suggest we start?"

"Most call me 'Wolf.' If they are wanting to hide out, it's a good guess they're headed northwest. They wouldn't want to be seen on the main roads, and not many wagons stray too far off. It's clear they abandoned the buckboard, but till they did we might pick up some wagon tracks. I say when we get to the edge of town we spread out and sweep the land between the Taos road and the Rio Grande on the west. There's another creek coming from the north before it dumps into the Rio Grande further south. If they were in a hurry, I don't think they would have crossed it, but if they did, there would be deep tracks at the crossing."

Except for his favored shin-high moccasins, Wolf wore cowhand garb and a Plainsman hat. Aside from being a neighbor and brother-in-law, Josh considered Wolf a close friend, and they had saved each other's lives a time or two. At just under six feet, Wolf was not as tall as Josh and not so much lean and lanky as thickly muscled with long legs.

"Josh, why don't you start near the Taos road, and I'll head toward the river. The marshal and Gabe can handle in between. If you see something that looks like recent wagon tracks, fire a shot in the air."

Josh figured Wolf would be firing the shot. He doubtless chose his own search position in the area where he expected to find the wagon tracks. He noticed a frown on Brig Paris's face that suggested he was chafing a bit at Wolf suddenly taking command. Wolf would step back some when the time was right, but he was confident about what he did best.

A half hour later, Josh heard a gunshot from the west in the direction of the Rio Grande. He reined Chief westward and headed across the rugged countryside which was essentially sand and rock at this location. Trees and brush began to appear as he neared the others who were gathered near a creek.

When Josh reached his fellow posse members, Wolf pointed toward the imprint of wagon wheels rolling along a seldom used trail that skirted the creek banks. They were not quite obscured by horse tracks.

Wolf said, "This has got to be the wagon. Not a heavy load but not an empty wagon box either. I'm guessing that a half dozen or so horses passed through later, likely the bank robbers trying to catch up to the wagon. I've been along this trail before. They will be forced to abandon the wagon within a mile, no more than two. The trees and brush get thicker by then, and even horseback riders are forced to go single file."

Paris said, "Well, let's keep moving then."

Less than a half hour later they came upon the wagon and empty coffin box. Josh said, "Mose will get his buckboard back, but he won't be happy about the trip out here to get it. It appears now he's just missing a mule."

Except for Wolf, who carried only a sheathed Bowie knife aside from the Winchester in its saddle holster, the others reached for their sidearms when they heard the crashing in the timber. Their six-guns were drawn and ready when the mule broke out of the woods and came up to the wagon.

Josh said, "It appears Andrew isn't deserting his post."

Gabe said, "What do we do with the critter?"

"I guess he comes with us," Wolf said. "He's haltered. We tie a rope to him and lead him. He might come in handy if one of the horses turns up lame and we are forced to convert the pack horse to a riding mount. This bunch is headed into the mountains. It's going to be slow going, and the critter won't hurt."

The deputy marshal said, "I ain't leading a dang mule."

"I'll lead Andrew," Josh said. "We're old friends anyhow."

Without a word, Wolf reined his horse into a break in the timber that he evidently found promising. Josh stayed behind to get the mule rope-haltered and then mounted his buckskin and headed out to catch up with the others, with Andrew tagging along on the lead rope.

Chapter 15

WILLI SPIEGELBERG SENT word to Marshal Calder as soon as he opened the envelope that had been slipped under the bank front door sometime during the night. It was the second night since the posse's departure, and he had no idea where Deputy Paris and his men might be by now.

When Calder arrived, he stepped out and waved the marshal into his office. When they were settled at Spiegelberg's desk, Willi pushed the note across the desk to Chance Calder who picked it up and read it aloud. "Mister banker: Bring $30,000 cash to Chimayo, at least half in gold. Rylee O'Brian will be turned over to you in exchange for the money. You must personally deliver. Alone. Delivery to be made May 30 at noon."

Spiegelberg said, "Chimayo. Isn't that a religious shrine north of here?"

"Close to twenty-five miles, I'd guess. A good day's ride through rugged country. I been there maybe ten years back. An adobe church and some Catholic shrines about. Place is said to have great healing powers, that's all I know. My people were Baptists."

"This is the twenty-eighth. I will work out arrangements for the money today. I will talk to my brothers. We cannot use bank funds, of course. I am not a great horseman and have little experience in the wilderness. I will need directions and a bit of guidance."

"Willi, you can't make that trip alone. I'm not sure you should go at all."

"I must. Rylee O'Brian is very special, and she would not face this dilemma if she were not an employee of the bank. And she stood up to those human parasites and refused to provide the vault combination."

"And they do not intend to allow her to live. Maybe just long enough for you to see her, but you are more likely to watch her die, and you will die with her."

Willi knew that, and he was afraid, but it was not in him to ignore the message. "I will deliver the money. If I go to this place, I assume I will receive further instructions."

"Do you know Cal Rivers?"

"Yes, I am acquainted with most of the Rivers family."

"Cal and a few ranch hands showed up in town last night with a horse herd to sell to Fort Marcy. He heard about the robbery and the abduction of the women. He was thinking about trying to catch up with Josh, but you might have better use for him."

"But the message says I must go alone."

"Cal is an old Army scout, and he has been in and out of as much trouble as most men see in a lifetime. I am going to run him down and ask him to talk with you. He can be a bit of a roughneck, but since he quit the bottle and made up with his wife, he's mellowed some. He scouted for the Army during the Comanche wars, and there ain't a better man to have with you in a gunfight. Some folks underestimate him because of his past rowdy ways, but he's so smart he even knows what a cow says to her calf. I'm going to send Cal by. Talk to him. Lay it all out. See what he says. And listen."

After Marshal Calder departed, Willi went to the mercantile to meet with his brothers about the ransom money. As he had suspected, Levi and Jacob backed him, and Emanuel and Lehman grumbled but agreed that family capital could be used to fund the ransom. He hoped that he might somehow return to Santa Fe with both the money and Rylee, but he figured he would be fortunate to return not slung over a horse's back. All his brothers had protested his venturing out alone.

When he returned to the bank, he found Cal Rivers, long legs stretched out, dozing in one of the waiting area chairs. He stopped at the chair, and said, "Calvin?"

Cal opened his clear blue eyes, straightened in his chair and looked up at the banker and instantly offered the sheepish grin that was his trademark. Shaggy, wheat straw-colored hair crawled from beneath his tattered round-brimmed Plainsman hat and stopped low on his neck. "Howdy, Willi. Marshal says you'd like to talk a spell."

"I would take it kindly if you would spare me a few minutes."

"Willi, as I recollect, me and Erin and the Circle M owe this bank near twenty thousand dollars. I can spare a day if you want it."

"Come on into my office." Cal stood to follow Willi, and at nearly four inches over six feet, towered over the short banker. As they sat down at the bank president's desk, Willi cast his eyes over the man attired like a saddle tramp with scuffed boots, holey faded blue jeans and well-worn flannel shirt. But he knew Cal had some money of his own deposited with the bank sufficient to cover the ranch debt.

The Circle M Ranch on which their horse and cattle business thrived these days was his wife's inheritance and titled in Erin's name. The pair, after some years of estrangement, had reconciled, but Cal was obviously taking no chances in case things turned sour again.

Willi dispensed with small talk. "Did the marshal tell you about the ransom demand?"

"Yep. Wondering how they got the note to you considering they're on the run."

"I hadn't thought about that."

"Somebody working on this end," Cal said. "Might be more than one. You determined to pay the ransom money?"

"I am."

"You might get as far as Chimayo before they take it. Might not. Of course, they'll try to kill you either way."

"You don't think they intend to make the exchange?"

"Nope. If the posse don't catch up with that outfit first, those women are dead."

A wave of nausea and weakness rippled through Willi's stomach. "Even if it's one chance out of a hundred, I've got to take it."

"Unless they're sending smoke signals back and forth, there ain't a chance that the men who got the ladies even know anything about taking Rylee to Chimayo."

"What would you do?"

"First, don't take the money. Sheets of paper and pennies maybe for the satchel. That said, I think you should take me along."

"But they said to go alone."

"Don't. We'll leave at different times and I'll circle around and meet you about five miles up the trail. Along the way, I can be checking to be sure no bushwhackers are waiting. I don't think they'd try to take you out close to town. They may even have things all planned out for Chimayo, but I don't want to take any chances."

"So what if they do have Rylee?"

"They ain't going to have the whole gang there. I'm guessing one or two men, no more than three. My Peacemaker will take them out, and Rylee will come home with us. Not much chance of it, though. I'm concerned about her, too."

"Well, if she's not offered for ransom, there's not much I can do."

"But maybe I can."

Willi could not see how, but Cal Rivers was something of a legend around Santa Fe, sober or drunk. He hoped that rumors Cal was now a confirmed teetotaler were true. He preferred the sober version of the man if lives were at stake.

"You will need to tell me what I should take on this journey."

"Again, bring an empty satchel for the money. Just get something else stuffed in it to look like there's money."

"But they will be expecting the gold and cash. I have arranged for the money."

"If they kill us, do you want the devils to walk away with the cash?"

"Well, no."

"I'll stop by the mercantile and get whatever we need, maybe talk to Mose about renting a pack mule. You just worry about your own things, bedroll, clothes and such. I'll see if I can get a few pup tents. I'd like to ride out tomorrow shortly after noon. We'll set up camp around dusk, hopefully a few miles away from Chimayo, so we can get there easily before noon."

"Are there people around Chimayo?"

"There are no more than a dozen small adobe houses scattered about. Mexican farmers and a man and woman the Catholic church hires to care for the property There's a general store about the size of your office with a six-horse stable attached, several barns with the houses. A person can also rent a shack for a night or two behind the store. A man's got to bring his own woman, though, if you know what I mean."

Willi did not want to think about it. He was certain religious rites were not being conducted in such a shack. "There's a priest?"

"Not the last I knew. One shows up every month or two I guess to do whatever priests do at a Catholic service. My folks claimed to be Methodists, but there wasn't no church within several days ride of the Slash R, so I don't know that much more about Methodists. Erin saw that we got Willow and Zack baptized at a church in Cimmaron, though, by a circuit-riding preacher. She sort of looks after the religious side of things in the family."

"Very well, so you will meet me some distance up the trail. How do I find this trail and keep from getting lost?"

"You just take the road to Taos till you meet up with me. I'll be waiting along the roadside and lead you to the Chimayo trail. It's not much of a trail. A wagon can make it through a tunnel of timber if the driver doesn't get pushed off the seat by tree limbs. Easy enough on horseback. I don't think there's much chance of attack on the Taos road—too much activity. If they don't wait till Chimayo, it will be on that trail."

Willi was a merchant and banker, not a warrior. This would be a new experience he would be more than willing to forego.

Chapter 16

IS BACK PROPPED against a tree in an aspen
grove just off the Taos road, Cal dozed off and
on while he awaited the arrival of Willi Spiegelberg. His bay gelding and pack mule were tethered in
a clearing upslope no more than twenty yards distant,
where he had found a lush patch of ungrazed grass. It
was late afternoon, and he figured Willi Spiegelberg
should be arriving soon.

He did not worry about catching a little shuteye during his wait. During his years of scouting, he had honed
an instinct that informed him when anyone approached.

Less than fifteen minutes later, his instincts alerted
him and the hair on the back of his neck bristled. He
sensed the presence of someone in the neighborhood,
and it was not Willi. He did not move but inched his hand
toward his old, holstered Peacemaker.

The visitor was off to his left crashing through the trees like a lame bull. Perfect location for slipping his six-gun out and firing a shot. He listened and waited, satisfying himself there was only one man. Soon he could make out a figure stumbling through the thick growth of aspen and juniper. Surely, he did not delude himself he was moving in with stealth. Cal got to his feet and had the Peacemaker in his hand now aiming the weapon at the man in the trees. "Stop where you're at, mister, or you're a dead man. Lift your hands over your head."

Compliance was instant. "Now walk out of the trees so I can get a better look at you."

The intruder stepped into the clearing, and Cal saw he was dealing with someone who was more boy than man, maybe seventeen or eighteen years old. Slender, medium height and a patchy attempt at a light brown beard that was more fuzz than hair. Pale blue eyes stared at the gun aimed at his chest, and the terror in the young man's eyes said that despite the pistol slung low on the kid's hip, Cal was dealing with no gunfighter.

"Take that pistol grip with thumb and one finger, lift it out of your holster and drop it on the ground."

"Yes, sir." He slowly removed his gun from the holster and dropped it at his feet.

Cal lowered his pistol and holstered it, unconcerned about the possibility the young man might go for his. The kid would likely shoot himself in the foot. "Now, what's your name, boy?"

"Uh, Marcus. Yeah, Marcus."

"Marcus what?"

There was a prolonged silence. "Little. Marcus Little."

The name was concocted, of course, but it did not matter. "That's what you want on your tombstone then?"

Little's eyes widened like they were on the verge of bursting. "You going to kill me?"

"That depends."

"Depends on what?" Marcus Little asked, his voice shaky.

"If you tell me the truth."

"About what?"

"To start with, about why you were headed my way."

"I just wanted to see who you was. I was riding by, and I could make out some critters through the trees up there on the slope. Wondered who they might belong to. Thought they might be strays."

"So you're a horse thief by trade?"

"No, no, sir. I don't steal no horses, but if they was strays, I figured to try to find the rightful owner. Now if I couldn't I'd make a home for the poor things."

"I guess I'll have to kill you. But don't worry none, I'll make a home for that stray horse of yours hitched off the road to the south of here I reckon. You prefer a bullet or hanging? I'm willing to accommodate either one."

"Look, I don't mean no trouble. I'll just walk away from here and go on about my business."

"You ain't told me about your business. You've till I count to five. One...two...three..."

"Hold up. I'll tell you why I'm here."

"Spit it out, kid."

"I don't even know who you are, but you ain't the fella I was looking for. He must've got way ahead of me somehow. He's a little old guy carrying a satchel. I seen him in Santa Fe going in the stable where I was keeping watch. He never come out, and I went in and asked old Mose what happened to him, and he says he don't know what I'm talking about. I think the fella went out the back and old Mose was covering for him. Anyhow, I knew where the guy was headed, so I took this road to try to get him in sight."

Good for Willi. He must have guessed he might be followed. He likely had not left yet when young Little inquired, and Mose was helping him cover his tracks. Little rode out ahead of him.

"I'll tell it to you straight, Mister Little. I'm waiting for the man you were following. As you probably know, he is Willi Spiegelberg, president of the Second National Bank of Santa Fe. Were you hired to kill him?" Little appeared genuinely shocked by the question.

"No, hell no. I ain't no hired gun."

Yet, Cal thought. "Then what are you?"

"I'm a messenger, that's all. Spiegelberg's meeting some fellers at Chimayo. Never been there, but I got me a sketch for directions. After that meeting, somebody's going to give me a satchel or bag with a message to take back to my boss."

"And who might your boss be?"

"You're asking me to put a lead slug in my head."

"Not if you get out of Santa Fe and head someplace else, learn a lesson maybe and take up honest work."

Little sighed. "I answer to a man named Paddy at the palace."

"What palace?"

"That castle thing that some guy that calls himself a prince put up. I stay there with some others in a wing off the stable that's sort of a bunkhouse. So far, all they let me do is be what they call a courier, get word to different places with instructions from Paddy and report back. I'm a good rider, and because of my age folks tend not to pay much attention to me. Anyway, that's what Paddy told me."

"What's going to happen to Mister Spiegelberg when he delivers this bag?"

"Ain't my concern. I got nothing to say about it."

"It's your concern if you are participating in a murder. If I turn you over to the U.S. Marshal, you could be swinging on the gallows."

"I'm not ready to die. Tell me what I got to do."

"I'll let Willi Spiegelberg decide. He's coming up the road now." He picked up Little's gun and shoved it in his belt. "Sit down and stay put."

He walked the short distance to the roadside and stepped out and waved. "Willi, up this way."

The banker approached astride a small sorrel mare that Cal judged to be a sturdy but docile animal. He could not imagine Willi trying to handle a spirited horse like his own bay, appropriately named Spirit, that was inclined to challenge on occasion.

When Willi reached him, the banker said. "I was confused. I saw a horse tied just off the trail not far back. I thought that might be yours."

"Nope. A guest. Dismount and come on back to meet him."

"Lordy, if I get down, I don't know if I can mount again. It's been years, if ever, since I've been in the saddle this long."

"I'll help you get back up if need be." Cal stepped over to lend a shoulder to help the banker dismount and half caught him when he slid off the mare's back.

Willi caught his breath and then leading the sorrel followed Cal back into the trees. When he saw Marcus Little sitting on the ground, he recognized the young man immediately. "I've seen this rascal. He's the one who was following me in town. I suspected he was up to no good. How did he come to be here?"

"I guess you tricked him at the stable. He thought you got ahead of him and then he caught sight of my horse and mule upslope and figured you were in here someplace and tried to sneak up on me. Let's say he needs work on his stalking skills."

"He planned to kill me?"

"Says not, but I don't know what he expected to do when he found you, I think he may be addled some." He could see Little seething now.

"What do we do with him?"

"I thought of hanging or just a slug in the head, but I'm thinking we need to save him for the marshal."

"Yes, by all means, he should be turned over to the law."

Willi was short on sense of humor, Cal thought, and squirmed at the notion of committing violence on the kid. "We'll do that. He might be a valuable witness when the dust settles on this business."

Little spoke for the first time since Willi's arrival. "I ain't talking, and if you claim I told you anything, I'll deny it."

"Suit yourself. I don't give a dang if you hang or not."

Willi said, "So what now. Should we be moving on?"

"Nah, we've got plenty of time to make it to Chimayo by noon tomorrow. We'll move up closer to my critters and stake your mare out with them. Good grass and a stream up there. We'll put up a couple of pup tents I brought along, start a fire and set up camp. No tent for our guest, but he'll do fine under the stars hitched to a tree."

"Will we need to take turns standing watch?"

'Nah, I ain't worried about that. Horses will tell us if company comes, and I don't miss much. And any trouble is likely going to be closer to Chimayo or at the site itself."

"I just want this to be over."

"Take it a day at a time. We'll be on our way back to Santa Fe this time tomorrow, but we'll likely have another night out unless we ride late."

"I'd be more than glad to ride late if I can sleep in my own bed tomorrow night."

"We'll see how things go." Cal, always a realist, knew that both men could be sleeping their final sleep before this time tomorrow.

Chapter 17

C AL CRAWLED OUT of his blankets the instant a hint of sunrise slipped over the low mountaintops to the east. Willi appeared to be snoozing in his tent, probably after a near sleepless night, and even Marcus Little, his wrists anchored behind his back around a small tree slept. When he retrieved the kid's gray gelding, Cal had found his bedroll and wrapped it around him as best he could, but blankets lay crumpled on the ground about him, his immobile hands being unable to pull them up.

Nonetheless, the young man slept, his neck bent forward and chin resting on his chest. He, too, had likely snatched little sleep, but Cal figured it would help beat down his will to resist.

He got the fire started, deciding he would use the Dutch oven he had hitched to the mule to bake biscuits, and, perhaps, fry up some bacon. A pot of coffee was high priority, of course. He was anxious to start the day since sleep had not eluded him last night.

The biscuits were about finished baking when a voice came from the edge of camp. "I got to piss."

Cal turned to his prisoner. "Go ahead."

"In my britches?"

"I don't give a dang." He walked over to the tree and unbound Little's wrists. "Go ahead and do your business. Just don't get out of my sight. A slug from my Peacemaker would catch up to you real quick if you tried to run."

"I ain't running. Where the hell would I run to?"

"Good point. When you're finished, come on over by the fire and pour yourself a cup of coffee. I'll have biscuits and bacon quick-like. Got some strawberry jam you might like."

"You're going to feed me?"

"Yep. I'd feed a stray dog. You don't rank that high in my book, but I got some hope for you."

He heard a moan from Willi Spiegelberg's pup tent. Now what?

He went over to the tent and peered in. "Willi, are you okay?"

"I may be dying."

"You're talking. You ain't likely dying."

"I can't move my legs without excruciating pain in my back. Maybe I'm paralyzed."

Willi's feet faced the tent opening, and Cal knelt to test the man's legs. He pinched the skinny calf of the right leg.

"Umm."

"Hurt?"

"Yes."

"You're not paralyzed."

Then off to his left side out of the corner of his eye, he saw a shadow pass him and sensed movement he turned and saw Little racing toward the other pup tent, where Cal had stashed the young man's weapons to keep them within his own easy reach. "Stop. Don't be a fool," he yelled.

By the time Cal got to his feet, the young man had the six-gun in his hand and swung around to fire. "Sorry, mister."

Cal dropped to the ground just before the gun fired, the shot echoing through the hills. Cal had his Peacemaker out now as Little lowered his gun for another shot. Cal squeezed the trigger, driving a slug into the center of the young man's chest. Little opened his mouth as if to say something, stumbled a few steps back and toppled over. Cal fought back the urge to vomit, sickened by the thought of killing a youngster, one he judged as more foolish than evil.

"Cal, what happened? Are you all right?"

"I'm okay, Willi. The kid tried to kill me. I had to shoot him."

"Is he dead?"

"I haven't checked yet, but I'd almost guarantee that he's dead or on his way. I didn't want to do it." He got up and stepped over and examined the prone figure on the ground. Little stared skyward with glassy eyes, a shocked look fixed on his pale face. He was not the first man Cal had been forced to kill in his adventurous life, but this one would haunt him. Most that he had taken down, he had never met or conversed with. They were strangers. Many were Indians, engaged in warfare and intent on taking his life or the lives of comrades. He had liked this kid and held out hopes for him, and this one was nearly enough to make him put down the gun. Of course, he would not.

He returned to the tent where Willi Spiegelberg lay. "Okay, Willi, you're not paralyzed. You've got a kink in your back from too many hours in the saddle, especially when you're not used to it. I've had this problem before. We've just got to get you up and moving around."

He crawled into the little pup tent and scooted behind Willi who lay like a turtle on its back. "I'm going to put my hands under your shoulders and lift you very slowly so you're sitting up. It may hurt some, but we've got to get you off your back."

"Oh, Lord. How did I ever get into this predicament?"

"You'll be fine." He started lifting and released one hand to push the man's upper back.

"Oh. Ah. Oh."

Willi was upright now. "Now, catch your breath and then we're going to turn you and get you on your hands and knees, so you can crawl out of here. Then I'll lift you to your feet."

In another fifteen minutes, Willi walked slowly and stiffly about the campsite, wincing with each cautious step and moaning with a misstep. Cal knew movement was painful, but they did not have a choice. Willi had to be back in the saddle soon.

Willi ate a biscuit standing up and declined the bacon. Cal ate and then tossed water on the remains of the smoldering coals. He took down the tents and rolled up the occupants' blankets and wrapped Little's body in his blankets. "We'll tether Little's horse and the pack mule here and decide later whether to bury the kid or tote the body back to Santa Fe."

"How can you remain so calm about this?"

"Never thought about it, I guess. Don't think of myself as calm. Just dealing with what life throws at me. Sometimes, it's fun. This ain't so much. Now let's get you back in that mare's saddle."

"I am not looking forward to this."

"By noon, it will all be over." Cal thought his remark could be taken different ways, but he figured it was true enough.

Shaded by a canopy of overhanging tree branches, the banker and former scout rode easterly from the Taos road down a rutted wagon trail that was fighting a battle against encroaching trees and undergrowth. Obviously, Cal thought, Chimayo was not a popular destination. There would be dozens of hideaways along this trail from which to launch an ambush. A glance at Willi Spiegelberg told him that every rocking of the saddle sent stabs of pain down his back and legs. The man was uncomplaining, but it was only a matter of time before he tumbled from the saddle.

He signaled a halt, and as they reined in their mounts, Cal said, "Can you shoot that Winchester in your scabbard?"

"My marksmanship would fall short of that of a man like yourself, but I can fire the weapon and hit my target sometimes—if it's not moving."

"That'll do. If you get a shot off, I'd likely hear you from a good distance up the trail."

"I don't understand."

"I am going to help you off the mare and get you situated off the trail a bit, and then I am going to hitch your horse in the trees on the opposite side. You will stay here, and if I don't return by midafternoon, you should get to that horse and find a way to get on somehow and then make your way back to Santa Fe."

"But I must deliver the money."

"Which doesn't exist. I'll take the satchel. I'm betting that will draw them out. If not, I'll ask around. Strangers will be noticed by the few folks who live in Chimayo."

"It doesn't seem right."

"Willi, I'm looking out after myself. Whoever's after the money is more likely to take me down if I'm trying to protect you, too. If I'm just worrying about my own skin, I'll be a tougher target and can maneuver the way I want. Think about it."

Willi nodded. "Yes, I suppose you're right. I should not have even made this journey."

"You were trying to help Rylee. Don't be hard on yourself. It's just not going to work out. Now, let's get you off that horse."

After Willi was positioned behind some junipers and undergrowth and his horse hitched to a tree across the trail, Cal continued his journey. When the church came into sight at the end of the near tunnel of woods that encased the trail, he reined in and dismounted. The church should be not much more than a half mile distant, he thought. He dismounted, led his gelding off the trail and into the trees, where he hitched the animal to a small tree limb that would break easily enough if the rider did not return. Even if the horse broke free, Cal was confident it would not stray far quickly.

He took the money satchel and began walking slowly off the trail's edge toward the church known by some for the healings that took place there. He carried his rifle in his other hand. His eyes scanned the trees lining the trail as he walked, noting that birds and squirrels in the branches seemed unperturbed, although a few scattered at his appearance. The instant he stepped into the cleared tract that harbored the church and nearby residences and other buildings, a rifle's crack sent him lunging into the woods.

A deep voice bellowed, "Throw down your gun, stand up, and state your business."

He thought the voice was coming from one of twin belltowers that fronted the church, but he could not be certain. "I won't stand up or throw down my gun, but I will state my business. I'm representing the Second National Bank of Santa Fe, and I bring money for the ransom of Rylee O'Brian."

"Spiegelberg was to do that."

"He is very ill. He could not, and I was sent in his place."

"Don't sound right. You're up to something."

"I'll toss my money satchel out as far I can into the road that runs toward the church." He stood, chanced stepping out of the trees a moment and heaved the bag some twenty-five feet out before darting back into his wooded cover. Nobody could pick it up without coming within easy range. Cal saw movement in the belltower to his left.

"What in the hell kind of throw was that? You carry it out so it's closer to the church. I'll tell you when to stop."

"With all the gold weighing it down, I couldn't throw it any farther, and I'm sure as hell not going to carry it to you, at least not until I have seen Rylee O'Brian. Prove you have the young woman with you, and then we can talk details of an exchange."

Two more rifle shots erupted from the belfry. The shooter certainly had never been an Army sniper, Cal thought. Neither shot came within five feet of the target, both high and wide according to the spray of wood chips from the aspen trees a few yards from his spot. Cal decided not to return the fire and to just wait for a spell. The gunman's sort was generally not proficient at the waiting game. A few minutes of silence and inaction would begin to gnaw on the man's brain, and he would make a foolish move.

But there should be a second man. He could not imagine that the person who was bossing this effort would send a lone man to carry out the task. Even though Willi Spiegelberg might not have seemed a formidable foe, this kind generally did not like one on one. Besides, one man might seem more likely to abscond with the money.

With that thought, Cal backed away, moving deeper into the woods, temporarily out of earshot as he started to circle the little village which was eerily still. He supposed gunfire sent everyone into hiding. When he next approached the clearing, he was nearer the church and off to the side of the shooter, who was focused on the direction of where the satchel lay. It would be an easy shot to take the man down now, but he waited on the edge of the clearing and watched.

Soon, the shooter hollered, "Hey, Bender, where are you?"

A short, spindly man stepped out from the spot where Cal had been when he tossed the satchel into the clearing in front of the church. "Down here. The feller was here. Found an empty shell. Ain't seen signs of a horse. I think he hightailed it out."

"Ain't likely. Go out and pick up the bag and bring it to me."

"Ain't so sure I want to do that."

"Why the hell not? You said you think he lit out."

"Well, yeah, but a feller can't be sure."

"Do it," the man in the belfry yelled.

The short man emerged from the trees, head swiveling from side to side and his movement deliberate and wary. He carried a rifle at the ready in his arms, the barrel following the direction of his search. Cal raised his Winchester to firing position and aimed. When the man was nearly ten feet from the bag, he fired two quick shots that kicked up dust in front of him. The man turned and aimed his rifle in Cal's direction. No more warnings. Cal planted lead in the gunman's chest with the next shot, and without waiting for him to fall whirled around, levering another cartridge into the chamber, and fired at the belfry shooter, repeating another time before the bushwhacker pitched forward and tumbled out the opening, rifle racing with him to the ground.

Cal stepped out into the clearing now, and without checking on the men he had just taken down, walked down the trail to retrieve his gelding. When he returned, he led the horse to a little adobe building that had a Spanish sign on it that he assumed designated it as a general store. Unlike many Anglos in the Southwest, he had never learned more than a few Spanish words and did not intend to. He was almost fluent in Comanche, however, since his stepdaughter, Willow, was half Comanche, and the language had been useful in his scouting days.

He noticed a few people were emerging from their homes now and that the village was returning to life. He hitched the horse to one of the hitching posts in front of the store and went inside, surprised to find a well-stocked and neatly organized establishment that contrasted with the drab exterior. The frontage of the store was narrow, giving the impression of a tiny store but the depth was substantial and allowed for a range of merchandise. His nose told him there was a brewing operation hidden somewhere in the rear of the building or perhaps in a cellar. He wondered if this enterprise might not be the key to the building's success. There was nothing illegal about a brewery in the territory, but sale to Indians was another matter, and just to the north in the Taos area, Pueblos prevailed in the population.

A reformed drunk himself, he was not judging anybody. He had a job to finish so he could get home. He was going to have a lot of explaining to do to his wife, Erin McKenna Rivers, as it was. They were a long way from establishing trust between them, but he could swear upon the Holy Bible that he had touched neither a drop of liquor nor another woman on this journey.

A lean Mexican stood behind a long counter off to Cal's right looking at him with appraising eyes. The man had a carefully trimmed mustache that curved around the corners of his lips and met up with a goatee. His demeanor was calm, and he showed no uneasiness at the sudden appearance of an Anglo visitor.

Cal walked up to the counter and found himself towering over the man. Of course, at six feet, four inches tall, he towered over most. "Hello, senor. Do you speak English?"

"Do you speak Spanish?"

"You just heard one of the five words I know." The man's speech was not accented, and Cal knew instantly he had stepped in cow shit again.

"Then we shall speak English. How may I help you?"

"I just killed a couple of fellers out in the village commons."

"Yes, I noticed. I think the least you could do is remove the bodies. It would be nice to spare the children such ugliness."

"Exactly. That's what I wish to do. Do you have any idea where those men hitched their horses? I want to haul the bodies back to the U.S. marshal in Santa Fe."

"Then you are not an outlaw?"

"Might depend on who you talk to, but I don't think of myself as such."

"The horses are in my stable behind the store. I can show you. I can furnish good binding rope for the bodies and will help you with the task if I may keep the saddles for stable rent."

"Sounds like danged steep rent, but it ain't nothing to me. I guess that's okay. You didn't happen to see a young woman with these men, did you?"

"Just the two rode in acting like they owned the place. Of course, we are not an organized town and have no law-man here. That makes men like these quite brave." The Mexican extended his hand, and Cal, at first surprised, accepted a firm grip. "We have a deal, my friend. My name is Rodrigo Navarro. I served in the Confederate Army with Marshal Chance Calder. Give him my regards when you see him."

"Cal Rivers."

"Of the Slash R Rivers?"

"My pa and brother Nate run the place."

"I know Levi. A good man."

Cal was ready to close the idle talk. "Well, I better get those horses and load my cargo."

Late morning the next day, Cal and Willi Spiegelberg reined in at the marshal's office in a wing of the federal courthouse. They were trailed by a mule and three horses bearing bodies slung and hitched over their backs.

Chance Calder stepped out of his office and surveyed the scene. "Looks like you fellers have been busy, but I don't see Rylee."

"Nope. Like I figured, they didn't have her."

"Smells like your friends are plenty ripe. Why don't you take them over to the undertaker."

"I assume Spiegelberg's," Willi chimed in.

"Why sure. You helped bring in the business, you folks ought to get to finish the work. You'll have to settle for what the county pays, though."

The Spiegelberg family operated a funeral parlor with their furniture store adjacent to the mercantile.

Cal said, "Willi, why don't you check in at the bank and then head home and get rested up. I'll see to the bodies and then come back and give Chance a full report."

"I would take that kindly, Cal. Thank you for your services. I'm certain I owe you for your time and effort. Stop by the bank in a day or two, and we'll settle."

"You owe nothing, Willi. I've got family involved in this. I've got a stake, too."

Willi reined his horse toward the bank, and Cal turned to the marshal. "I met a Mexican feller, Rodrigo Navarro. Said he served in the war with you."

Calder chuckled. "Yep, Roddy. He's from an old land grant Spanish family. Went to that fancy school back east. They call it Harvard, I think. I don't why in the hell he came back to enlist in the war. They generally weren't calling up the Mexicans, but a good number volunteered. Roddy mostly collected guns and valuables off dead or wounded Union soldiers and sold the stuff. He must have made a small fortune. Problem was it was all Confederate dollars, so it was worthless the way the war turned out."

Chapter 18

"BAD NEWS, BOSS," Paddy O'Meara said when he walked into Charles Hanover's office.

Hanover looked up from his desk, eyes narrowed, and lips pressed tight. He glared at O'Meara a few moments before he spoke. "Well, what the hell is it?"

"The banker and some big fella paraded through town an hour or so ago, leading three mounts with bodies slung over their backs. One was your messenger kid Billy Rider, and the others were the men that were supposed to ambush Spiegelberg and make off with the ransom money. It's plenty clear they didn't get the money if Spiegelberg was even fool enough to take it."

Hanover seethed. "Spiegelberg could not have done this. Who is the big man you are talking about?"

"Word is that his name is Cal Rivers. Brother to the fella that went out with the posse. They come from a big ranching family up north of Taos. Home place is in the mountain foothills. Ain't folks to mess with, I'm told."

Hanover needed a drink. His hands were trembling, and he grasped the end of his desk so O'Meara could not see. "We've got to get this cleaned up quick. My wife and kids will be here in less than a week. I want things calm by then. Earlene senses when things aren't right and pushes me for answers. She's already suspicious about the source of our money and has started asking too many questions. She wears a cross on a chain around her neck. Big on praying about things. She's a God-fearing Baptist, and her stuffy old man back in Illinois has got money and political influence. She won't starve if she leaves me and takes the kids."

"Maybe you ought to just let her go."

"Oh, I would, but I want my kids, Charles Junior, anyhow. She can have the girls. Junior, though, as the eldest son, is my rightful heir. Besides, she would be after my money if we divorced." It occurred to him that if misfortune should visit Earlene, and she died, that problem would die with her. He could employ a nanny to care for the kids, a pretty one perhaps whom he might bed on occasion.

O'Meara said, "I'll leave you to figure out what to do about your wife. For what it's worth, I always found her to be a kind and gracious lady. Do you want anything done right now?"

"How many men do we have available at the castle?"

"Twelve counting me. The number changes, though, because we send men out to contact the other outfits working for you."

"I want a man in the watchtower twenty-four hours a day to warn us if hostile forces approach. Close and lock the entrance gate and the big doors."

"You're worried about the law?"

"The Army's nearby. The marshal might summon their support."

"They're damned careful about getting involved in civilian affairs. I don't think that's much to worry about."

"Just do what I tell you. I want men on alert and ready to go to the parapets to defend this place if the need arises. And the women hostages. You gave the orders, didn't you?"

"Yeah, but I didn't like it. The Chandler woman should have no more than a day to live. The bank lady has three if we don't send word to stop it. Time's short to get a message to the cliff dwelling. You might need a hostage."

"She's seen too much by now. She would likely be a dangerous witness. No, I don't think that so-called posse will be a problem. They'll return like whipped pups. We just need to let this play out. We've had jobs that didn't work out before. When this quiets down, we'll move on to something else a good distance from Santa Fe."

"Whatever you say, Boss. I'll put out the alert and keep everybody close to home." O'Meara turned away and left the office.

With O'Meara gone, Hanover stood and started pacing the room, fingers interlaced behind his back. He should not have struck the Santa Fe bank. If it had not been for that arrogant Rylee O'Brian and her snooping, he would not have considered it. And then Jessica Chandler gets herself with child. Women had their uses, but it seemed they were more nuisance than pleasure in his life, and that included Earlene.

Chapter 19

RYLEE STUDIED THE circular pit-like structure where she and Jessica had been placed by their captors. No windows. Sandstone brick walls. Only exit through a circular opening at the top. They had arrived at ancient Indian cliff dwellings constructed beneath a huge sandstone overhang from a cliff wall above. Apartment-like structures, many crumbling away and walls caved in now, were backed against the wall, and she assumed the best of these had been appropriated by the outlaws.

Underground structures like their prison seemed to be located on the wide ledge in front of the dwellings. She believed she and Jessica were in what the Pueblos called a kiva, a gathering place for religious ceremonies and various meetings. Access was via a ladder which, of course, had been pulled up. She judged the opening to be eight to nine feet high, too far for her to reach and lift herself out. At five feet and nine inches tall, she was taller than most women and long armed, but she would not be able to leap high enough to grasp the opening's edge by more than her fingertips if that.

But there were fallen bricks scattered about the floor and other loose ones in the walls that could be removed. They could build a crude platform by stacking the bricks and add two or three feet to her reach. If she could pull herself out, she could lower the ladder for Jessica, and then they would run. Their race would all be downslope, sliding on the loose rock some distance till they reached solid footing and disappeared into the mountain forest.

There was another possibility. They might get supper. If so, one of two things would happen. Someone would bring it down the ladder, or he would drop it through the hole.

She explained her plan to Jessica, who resisted.

"I can't do this," Jessica said. "I will hold you back. I will help gather and stack the bricks, but I don't want to go."

"Jess, I overheard the men talking this afternoon. They are going to play poker tonight, and the winners get first chance at us. We will be raped again and again as the evening goes on. We will be killed soon, if not tonight, the next or the one after that. The sun will set in an hour. I smell smoke, so they are getting ready to fix supper. We need to get the bricks gathered, but we can't build the platform yet in case somebody lowers the ladder to bring our food down."

"But that person might see that we have gathered bricks."

"It doesn't matter because he will be dead before he gets word to anybody."

"I don't understand."

"When somebody comes, pretend you are ill. Lie down on the floor and moan pitifully. You are an actress. You can do it."

"Well, yes, I suppose so."

"If someone doesn't bring something to eat by dark, we go ahead with the bricks and pray nobody shows up. I'm sure the gambling will start not long after supper."

It was nearly dark, and Rylee was preparing to start stacking the bricks when she heard the shuffling of boots and rattling of small stones as someone approached the kiva.

"Okay, start now," Rylee said.

Jessica dropped to the floor, curled into a fetal position and commenced moaning.

A voice came from above. "What in the hell's wrong down there?"

Rylee said, "Jessica's sick. Real sick."

"Well, she'd better get over it. You ladies are going to be busy tonight."

Jessica commenced coughing and gagging and then began sobbing.

"You can't be that sick. I got one plate of venison and beans to split betwixt you. I'll let the ladder down and bring it to you, and I can check on the sick lady then."

Rylee thought, this is too good to be true. And the server was the short, stocky man with the bearded face and balding scalp, the man called Jackson. He had not appeared to be one of the quick-witted ones among the captors, although she guessed she could not say that about any of them.

Jackson lowered the rickety, rotting timber ladder. He grunted when he stepped onto the stone floor and handed the plate to Rylee before he bent over Jessica. She promptly set the plate down and lifted her cotton chemise that barely covered the holstered derringer. At least the confiscation of their dresses had made the weapon easier to reach.

Jackson said, "What's the matter with you, woman? You can't hurt that dang much."

Jessica did not have time to answer before Rylee grabbed the man by the chin, yanked him upright and pressed the derringer against his back.

"What the..."

She squeezed the trigger, and drove the lead slug into his back, the man's flesh muffling the sound significantly as she had hoped. The small caliber derringer was not a serious noisemaker anyway. He slid to the floor moaning. And she picked up one of the sandstone bricks and began pommeling his head till he was still and silent.

Jessica had clambered to her feet and was staring at Rylee in wide-eyed disbelief.

Rylee said, "Now get going up that ladder. Yell if you see anybody up there. I'm going to get this man's gun belt and Colt."

"I can't. I won't."

"You will if you want to give that child you are carrying a chance at life."

Jessica obeyed while Rylee removed Jackson's gun belt and cinched it about her own waist. It was plenty loose, but her hips held it up for now. She could work on punching a hole later, which reminded her to search for a penknife. She found one in his front pocket, picked up the plate of food and scurried up the ladder. She handed Jessica the knife, and her eyes searched the surrounding ruins. She saw the other men at the campfire at the far end of the dwelling site a good distance away, but in the moonlight, the captives could be easily sighted if someone was checking the area.

"Follow me," she whispered to Jessica. "Stay as low as you can and still move. We've got to get out of here."

Chapter 20

AS THE OUTLAWS finished supper and readied for the poker game, Hack Hackler noticed that Jackson wasn't present. "Where's Jackson?" he hollered.

The men stopped what they were doing, looking at each other and then craning their necks about as they attempted to sight their absent member. Tomcat spoke up, "He took a supper plate to the women earlier. I'm betting the son-of-a-bitch stayed on for a poke or two. No way he'd win an early one."

Calling on his youngest and least likely to kill Jackson for any transgression, Hackler said, "Richie, go see if Jackson's with the women. If he is, tell him to get his ass back here. Take one of the lanterns so you can see down in the damn pit."

Richie had been finishing supper by the fire and put his plate down and got to his feet. "I doubt if he's there, Boss. He probably walked off someplace to take a crap."

"And a man's allowed to do such things. Just check and report back."

Less than five minutes later, Hackler heard Richie's frantic yelling. "Hack, Hack, come quick. Trouble. Hack." What in the devil could the kid be screaming about?

Hackler raced toward the kiva with Tomcat close behind. When he arrived, he found Ritchie flat on his belly suspending the lantern through the kiva opening. The ladder was tossed off to one side.

"What's going on, kid?" Hackler said, kneeling beside him.

"I think Jackson's dead. The women are gone."

"Impossible." He laid down beside Richie and peered into the kiva. It was Jackson for sure. It looked like a bull had stomped his face in. "Tomcat, get the ladder and go down there and see if Jackson's still alive. Maybe he can tell us something."

"You sure them women are gone?"

"Do what I said, damn it. We got the place lighted up. They ain't there. Since when are you scared of a couple of women?" If there was a coward in the bunch it was Tomcat. He was tough and cruel with those he judged weaker but ran like a bat out of hell if he thought he was up against his equal or better. He never had liked the man and wondered how he ever ended up in the outfit.

When Tomcat reached the kiva floor and knelt by Jackson, he rolled the man over. "You won't believe this," he hollered. "Jackson's got a gunshot wound in his back. He's dead as a can of corned beef, and his head's ground up so bad you can't hardly tell who he is if you didn't know."

"Is his Colt down there?"

"I don't see it. And I'll be danged if his gun belt ain't gone, too. One of them bitches must know a thing or two about guns."

"Okay. Get back up here. We've got to get back to camp and figure out how to hunt the women down."

Back in camp with all the men clustered around the fire, Hackler spoke. "Forget about the poker game, boys, the prizes killed Jackson and escaped. We've got to track them down and either kill them or bring them back here. I'm thinking killing is best. If you do that, take their scalps and leave the bodies behind. Scavengers will clean them up fast out here. There is a bounty for each scalp or woman. One thousand dollars each. If two of you are together when the deed's done, you split it."

Moose, the tallest of the bunch, spoke up. "Hack, we ain't going to pick up nobody's trail in the dark. Besides, they're wearing next to nothing, they might freeze in the night chill before we find them."

"Not likely in one night, but if we find somebody dead, get that scalp. We need to prove they're dead to the higher-ups. We'll wait till sunrise. Then we'll break up into three groups by twos. First, we try to find a sign of where they headed out, my concern is they might circle around while we're chasing them and try to come back here for horses. Richie and me will hike down the trail we come in on to be sure they didn't head that way. If somehow, they got horses, they'd have to get past us, and we'd put a quick end to that foolishness. Anyway, after we're convinced they ain't taking the horse trail afoot, we'll come back here to watch the camp. We've got to keep a lookout for that posse, too."

Moose said, "I'm liking this less by the minute, Hack. I don't take to the notion of leaving my horse behind with prospects of a posse coming."

"We got no choice. If they headed into the mountain country below, you can't get your horse down there, and there's too many rough places a critter can't go. We're all going to be afoot till this is done. Signal with three gunshots if you get them. That sound will carry a long way in this country. When you hear that, head back, or if you're out three nights after this one, give it up. We might just all decide to disappear. Now get some shuteye. Put together what provisions you can carry in the morning and be ready to move out."

Hackler hoped the bounty was sufficient to get the men on the trail of the escapees. He had seen mostly hostile faces in the group, and he did not want to deal with a mutiny.

Chapter 21

GABE LAURENT WAS growing impatient. The posse seemed to be moving at a snail's pace, and he feared the abductors were outsmarting them. He did not doubt for a moment Oliver Wolf's skill as a tracker, but he was not fond of the deputy U.S. marshal who seemed inclined to challenge every decision Oliver made. The man, as the only official lawman, commanded the pursuers but did not listen well to others.

It was early afternoon of their second day out of Santa Fe, and even the deputy admitted now that they likely had not closed the gap with the outlaws. They had lost a good half day this morning when Oliver had tracked the riders into a shallow stream flowing down the mountain slopes. There had been no sign of horse tracks or dung on the other side, and it was obvious they had taken to the stream to eliminate any sign.

Deputy Paris had insisted the riders would have headed up the gentle slope toward an obvious hideaway in the mountains. Wolf was skeptical, suggesting the route was too obvious. He thought it more likely they headed downstream with the objective of exiting the water and moving on in a divergent route. He asked if he might check downstream while the others started upstream, but Paris had declared, "We stay together."

An hour out, Wolf turned back, telling Josh Rivers he would fire two shots if he came across anything. With riders trying to negotiate rocks, trees, and outcroppings on both sides of the stream, the followers were struggling and should remain within hearing distance of a gunshot. Wolf disappeared before Paris realized he was missing. Considering that Wolf was moving downslope over a route that had already been scrutinized, he made good time, and not more than another hour later the others heard two gunshots.

When Josh informed Paris, who was already angered by Wolf's desertion, that the shots meant the Cherokee had picked up the trail, Gabe thought the man might explode. His face had turned near scarlet, and his eyes simmered, but the man turned back.

They had found Wolf on the opposite side of the stream only twenty minutes downstream from where the deputy had made the bad choice. There was no question now that Wolf had become the de facto leader of the group, and now they awaited his words.

Josh said, "So, now what?"

Careful not to upset Paris further, Wolf said, "I followed the trail into the woods a short distance. At first it looked like they were heading back south, which made no sense. Then they turned suddenly west, and I'm betting we'll find them angling north before too long, pretty much in the direction the stream flows from, so Brig had us pointed right."

Gabe noticed he did not add that they never would have picked up the trail again following the deputy's course.

Wolf continued, "From the horse apples along the trail, I'm guessing we are more than a full day behind, but from here I don't think we have any choice but to keep following and hope we don't lose their trail someplace. With seven men and two women, that's at least nine horses, it's dang hard to move without leaving sign with that many critters. It's not like following one or two riders or somebody afoot," He turned to Paris. "What do you say, deputy?"

"Why don't you just lead the way for now. I'll say my piece when I need to."

Wolf reined his mount away from the stream, following the trail he had already explored. Paris fell in behind with Josh and Gabe bringing up the rear. As Wolf predicted, the trail eventually angled north, and the outlaws soon connected to a wider, more often used trail that allowed the pursuers to ride two abreast climbing into the high country.

As dusk approached, the men and horses needed rest, and Wolf pointed to a clearing not far from a spring that trickled from a sandstone cliff wall. Again, he turned to Deputy Paris. "What do you think?"

"About the only flat ground up in this country. It'll do. Looks like there's some grass out on the edge. That little stream that flows away from the spring ought to provide water for the horses. Let's tend to the critters and stake them out. Then we get a fire started and put some grub together. We'll grab some decent shuteye tonight and be saddled and ready to ride out at the first crack of dawn."

Gabe thought that the deputy was coming around some now that he saw Wolf wasn't trying to take over the show. It eased his mind now that some order had been returned to the search, but he worried about the lapse of time. Rylee and Jessica could already be dead by now, and he did not want to think about what the bunch of no-goods might be doing to them if they were alive.

Beans and coffee and biscuits. He liked all three well enough, but up to tonight they had enjoyed some ham or beef slices to go with them. He knew that morning would bring cold, crusty biscuits and hopefully some coffee again. When they were sitting around the fire finishing supper, he was surprised when Paris said, "Oliver, any thoughts for tomorrow?"

Wolf said, "We can't chance not following the sign they leave on their trail, but I think I know where they're headed."

The deputy's brow furrowed. "You do? Where?"

"Ghost Mesa. That's the English translation anyhow. Named for the ghosts that are said to roam the place. Cliff dwellings of ancient Pueblos, I'm told, before they moved to lower ground like Taos that lent itself better for farming and livestock and such."

Paris said, "Are you certain about this?"

"No. I'm not inclined to be certain about much of anything, but we'll know by midafternoon tomorrow. Whatever route they take they'll intersect with the Ghost Trail if that's where they're headed."

"Then we could reach them by tomorrow night?"

"Not likely. You don't want to be on that trail after dark. It starts wide and ends wide, but there are places in between that are so narrow only a single rider can pass over. A man would never get a wagon up there from the east for sure. There's another trail that comes in from the west that would allow a wagon, but we would be forced to circle around through canyons and mountains and lose another day, maybe two. We've just got to see where their trail takes us and how long it takes to get there. If I'm right about where they're headed, I'm guessing we'll be waiting till morning of the next day to move in."

Josh said, "And how long do you think it will take to get there after that?"

"A good three hours. That trail is like a dang corkscrew going up the sheer mountain face. Some places we'll want to walk and lead the critters. And the worst of it is we're not likely to surprise anybody—something to be thinking about."

Gabe thought about it a moment. "What if we left the horses behind and made the climb at night?"

Wolf looked at him. "We can be thinking about that, too."

Chapter 22

AT RYLEE'S INSISTENCE, Jessica picked at the food plate they had escaped with, but she ate no more than a few bites of venison and no beans, seemingly unwilling to eat more without a fork. Rylee ate what was left, virtually scooping the beans from the tin plate into her hand before dumping them into her mouth. She was hungry, and one of them needed to maintain her strength.

She had only a rough idea of their location, but the North Star told her they were roughly headed south, the direction she had chosen because of the ruggedness of the country that would make horseback pursuit nearly impossible. She would be better able to orient herself by the sun in the morning. Her goal was to find the Rio Chama, a tributary of the Rio Grande. She knew that when the rivers merged, she could follow the Rio Grande

to Santa Fe. The plan seemed simple enough, but she figured anywhere from fifty to eighty miles of some of the
ruggedest country in the territory stood between them
and their objective.

She hoped that once they reached the Rio Chama, they
might fashion a crude raft that would carry them downstream, although it was said that some places the river
was narrow but swift with white water racing through
steep sandstone canyons. She knew that nearer Santa Fe,
folks lived along the river, and some of the old mountain
men had cabins farther north and west into the highest
mountains. She hoped that she might come across help
sooner rather than later if they could reach the river.

Rylee was confident she could survive the journey. As
a ranch girl who had seen her father killed and her mother raped and murdered by Comancheros before being
abducted herself, she had dealt with adversity. After Jael
Rivers, then known among the Comanche as She Who
Speaks, rescued her, she lived for a time among the tribe.
She could do this. Her concern was Jessica and the un-
born child. She would not desert the woman. It was not
in her to do that.

They had stopped for a rest after hours of walking and
weaving through forest on high ground. Rylee wanted
the higher elevation if their captors caught up with them.

Her experience with pistols was limited, though, and she would certainly be no match for rifles. Right now, she might sell herself for a Winchester. She was confident she could hold off an army with a rifle.

Her feet hurt, and she suspected they were bleeding. She would try to deal with that at daylight. She looked at Jessica who sat on the ground resting her back against a tree trunk. The woman was exhausted. Rylee doubted if the outlaws would mount a search before sunrise. If she were alone, she would continue at least several more hours. She doubted Jessica could make ten minutes.

"Jess," she said, "I won't stray far, but I am going to see if I can find a place for us to bed down and grab some sleep for a few hours."

Jessica began sobbing. "I'm freezing. We don't have any blankets, and we're nearly naked. My feet are bloody. I can't take another step. I'm done. I can't go any farther. I just want to die. If you are truly my friend, you will shoot me and put me out of my misery."

"Jess..."

"I mean it. I'm not going. And if you don't kill me, I'll wait for those men to do it."

"You just need some rest. Now stay put. I will be back in a few minutes." She did not worry about Jessica running off somewhere, so she turned away and disappeared into the trees. She moved to lower ground, seeking something that might serve as temporary shelter, something for a windbreak. A chill was settling in now, and it would be downright cold before the night was finished. That was the way of the mountains. Tomorrow, if they could break into sunshine, they would warm quickly enough and likely be looking for shade by afternoon.

She stumbled on a rock and almost pitched over the edge of a bank or cliff. As she fought to regain her footing, she saw that she would not have fallen more than three feet, although with the rocky surface she could easily have broken a leg or arm or injured her head. Then it occurred to her that she had found their shelter. The bank tapered off to her left, sloping down to ground level and she carefully crept down. There was plenty of dead brush nearby and she started collecting it and laying it against the bank to make a crude lean-to. Grass was scarcer, but she pulled what she could and spread it on the stone floor, clearing loose stones as best she could.

She guessed that the project had taken her an hour, and she hurried back to where she had left Jessica, fearing several times that she was lost before finding the landmarks she had taken note of during her search for shelter. When she found Jessica, she saw that she had not moved an inch, but now her head was drooped forward, chin resting on her chest, eyes closed, and she slept soundly.

Rylee hated to waken her, but she knew that with the cold, sleep would be brief. "Jess. Jess, I'm back." She placed a hand on Jessica's shoulder and shook it gently.

Jessica woke, her eyes showing confusion as they darted about her surroundings. Then she looked up at Rylee. "What do you want?"

"I found a place to sleep, but you must walk just a short distance."

"I can't walk."

"You must, and you can. I will tend to your feet in the morning."

"Did you find a blanket?"

"No, of course not, but this will be warmer than out in the open. Now let me help you up." She took Jessica's hands and pulled her to her feet. "Now place your hand on my shoulder and lean on me as much as you need to."

They took the first steps very slowly, but as Rylee had suspected would happen, the pace began to increase. She had to assist Jessica over some rough spots and finally down the bank to their shelter. She helped Jessica into the brush shelter, positioning her closest to the bank where she would get the most wind protection.

When she crawled in, she said, "I want you to face the bank, and I am going to spoon up against you, and we will be each other's blanket."

Fortunately, Jessica was too exhausted to argue or ask questions. Five minutes after Rylee wrapped her arms around her and snuggled close, Jessica was sleeping again. Slumber did not come so easily for Rylee, but finally she surrendered to a cold and restless sleep.

Chapter 23

RYLEE WOKE SUDDENLY several hours before sunrise, having slept only intermittently before that time. She knew that any thought of capturing another hour or two of rest was hopeless. Her brain was working now. Too much to do, too many plans to make and problems to solve. She could not do much in the darkness, and she knew that Jessica needed the warmth of her body, so she decided to stay in place for a time. She was not all that anxious to crawl out of their shelter and venture out into the woods anyway.

Only minutes later she tensed when she heard someone—or something—moving through the brush outside the shelter. She sat up and reached for the Colt that rested in its holster beside her. The outlaws could not have caught up with them so quickly unless pursuit had started during the night, possibly immediately upon discovery of Jackson's body. But how would they have picked up their trail in the dark?

Suddenly, it was silent, no sound of movement. She could see nothing. The moonlight was efficiently blocked by the towering trees that surrounded them, and everything about the two escapees wore a shadowy, shroud of blackness. She waited. She heard heavy breathing now as the visitor drew nearer. A man would not make that much noise unless he had been running or climbed a steep slope, the latter of which would be possible here.

She could see the eyes now as it poked its head into the shelter, and then the cold nose touched her foot and sniffed. A bear. The blood, she thought. It would chomp her foot off to start. She had no chance against a wounded bear, so she pointed her Colt skyward and squeezed the trigger. The resulting explosion was deafening. Jessica awakened screaming, and she could hear the bear grunting as it crashed again through the brush in retreat.

"What happened?" Jessica said. "Have we been found?"

"It was a bear. I scared him off."

"Oh, my God. What next? If we don't freeze first, we'll be eaten by bears."

"I haven't heard about many grizzlies in these parts, mostly brown bears. Unless they're protecting cubs, they rarely bother people. Mostly they eat plants and berries and such, sometimes mice and insects. They'll eat dead creatures, and they might make a few meals of us if we're dead, but they don't hunt anything very big. They'll stay away from us if they see us."

"Of course, we're going to die, so sooner or later they'll have us."

Rylee scolded herself for the light remark about being bear meals. "We're not going to die. Now get that notion out of your head. We do need to move out soon. I've been thinking about something for our feet. I've got an idea."

"There is a trading post with shoes nearby?"

At least Jessica's sense of humor had not died, sarcastic as it was. "I am going to see if I can find some birch trees. I know we passed some last night. Then I will cut and peel off sections of bark for our feet. They peel easily and are somewhat flexible. We can line them with leaves and anchor them to our feet and ankles with strong, thin vines. Indians use birch bark for all kinds of things. They will protect our feet, and the leaves will pad the soles of our feet."

"You are insane. What do you want me to do?"

"At first light, you could look for strong vines. Avoid poison ivy. Do you know what that looks like."

"Three leaves. I got in some as a girl. Never again."

"Wild grape vines would be best. We have them in this area of the territory. I understand that many are descended from vines the Spanish planted here several centuries ago. Just see what you can find but don't lose sight of the shelter. I may come upon something while I am searching. If you find something, I can cut what we need with the penknife when I return."

Rylee departed feeling much better about Jessica's prospects and felt it would help her to contribute to their survival. She did not delude herself, however, realizing her mental and physical condition was fragile. She quickly found a small grove of young birch trees growing near a narrow mountain stream that raced over a rocky bed. It appeared clean and fresh and would provide a source of water to start their day.

This time of year, with snow still melting higher in the mountains, she did not anticipate water supply becoming a problem, but they needed to find the cleanest sources possible. Medical scholars had identified tainted water as a major cause of typhoid fever that had killed so many, especially Civil War soldiers and westward migrants, and they speculated that contaminated water might be the source of many illnesses.

The glow of morning sunrise crept over the horizon just in time for Rylee to commence her task. Her knife cut through the birch bark like a surgeon's knife into flesh, and she thanked the dead donor for keeping the blades sharp. When she had peeled ample bark, she returned to the shelter with her harvest.

She found Jessica enthused about finding what she thought were wild grape vines albeit no sign of grapes. She led Rylee down the slope a short distance to her find. Rylee agreed with her partner's identification. The leaves that had turned brownish and were starting to shrivel were clearly grape leaves, and the plant was a sickly specimen, but there were ample vines for her purposes.

An hour later, the morning sun was offering warm rays, and the women were outfitted with birchbark sandals with leaves for inner soles and wrapped and tied about their feet and ankles. It would take some time to become accustomed to them, but Rylee figured they were far superior to bare feet or boots. Like her foster mother, Jael Rivers, Rylee preferred moccasins for riding and walking.

They had no gear to collect other than the penknife Rylee now kept clutched in her left hand, the gun belt and holstered pistol, and derringer still cinched to her thigh, so they were ready to move on. Before departing, they dismantled the shelter, tossing the shrubs and branches back into the woods and scattered the leaves that comprised their bed about. Rylee knew they would not fool an experienced tracker about their presence there, but some men might not take notice.

An hour later, Jessica was again exhausted and in misery. To Rylee's annoyance her companion was not one to suffer in silence, and, consequently, she was never certain how seriously to take her complaints. They stopped to rest near a spring, where they could drink their fill. They would not outrun pursuers at this pace, and she just hoped the men lacked the persistence to make more than a token effort to find their quarry.

"I'm starving," Jessica complained, as they sat on boulders near the hillside spring.

This from the person who refused to eat the previous night. "We need water most and be thankful we have ample sources for that. We should keep our eyes open. Some shrubs are bearing edible fruit now, and there are plants that can be eaten, even insects."

"Bugs? I'll starve first."

"It's best to cook most, and I should be able to start a fire in a day or two. Flint is plentiful, and I should get sparks with the knife blade. Too risky now. I doubt if I can get near enough to hit an animal with a pistol shot, but we won't starve if we don't get too fussy about what we eat."

"I've got limits."

Rylee shrugged and got up. "We must move on."

"I'm slowing you down, aren't I?"

"You can't help it, but we'll be fine if we just keep our pace steady."

"I can't."

"You cannot if you don't try."

Jessica sighed and got up to follow.

Within another hour, Jessica dropped to the ground. She had lagged some fifty feet behind Rylee by this time, and Rylee turned back. If outlaws were trailing them, they would have narrowed the gap considerably by now. She had lost track of the times she and Jessica had stopped since the escape, and she felt a sense of hopelessness when she turned back to assist her companion.

When she approached, Jessica said, "I'm done. Leave your derringer with me and go on."

Rylee said nothing. If she left the derringer with its single remaining cartridge, Jessica might well use it on herself. Besides, she would not abandon her, and she did not intend to die. "What is the matter specifically. Your feet?"

"No, my feet are holding up. I'm just exhausted to my limit, and I am cramping something awful." She lifted her chemise. "And there is blood in my underpants. I guess I should take them off."

Rylee knelt and helped her slip out of the underpants. She had no experience with such things, but she suspected Jessica was losing the baby. "Let me get you near the big oak over here, so you have something to lean against."

No more than fifteen minutes later, Jessica groaned, reached between her thighs and momentarily displayed a bloodied object no larger than a strawberry in her hand. She started shrieking and crying. "My baby, my baby. My Juliet."

Rylee tried to wipe the tears from Jessica's cheeks. "I'm sorry, so sorry." She was speechless, though, when Jessica handed her the object and almost vomited when she saw the beginnings of a head and face forming in the little mass.

"Bury her. Cover her with stones, so the scavengers and bears don't get her."

Then Jessica moaned and fainted. Thankful for a bit of silence, Rylee took a stick and dug a small hole at the base of the tree and rolled a large stone over the site. She checked Jessica again and confirmed that her breathing was steady, before going to a nearby rivulet that was not yet a full-fledged stream where she washed her hands before rinsing out the underpants as best she could.

Evidently, Jessica had convinced herself that the baby was a girlchild and had named her Juliet. She wondered now if she should have pushed Jessica so hard to escape with her. She shook off the guilt some, however, by telling herself that to remain was a certain death sentence. Regardless, it was obvious they could not move on today, and it was increasingly likely that the hunters would run them down without any intent to drag them back to the cliff dwellings.

She decided that her best strategy was to prepare to meet them head-on. That was preferable to being caught by surprise. If only she had a rifle, she was confident she could keep them at bay, cripple or kill a few, and send them retreating. When she returned to Jessica, she found that she was awake but not entirely lucid.

"You buried Juliet?"

"Yes, of course. Only a few feet to your right. Where the big rock is."

"This is where I want to be buried. Will you do that?"

"I'm sorry for your loss, Jess, but now we must think of ourselves and living."

"I told you I don't want to live."

"So you want Prince Charles Hanover to win? Do you really want him to get by with this?" Revenge could motivate people, and she would use whatever tactics necessary to bring a desire to live back to Jessica.

There was a long silence before Jessica spoke. "I can't walk for more than a few minutes right now."

"We're going to make a stand here. I will help you upslope to that rock outcropping that overlooks the area below. I will give you my derringer and the penknife."

"I might fight off a toad with those."

"You use the derringer only if someone gets within arm's length of you. We'll position you behind the stones. If you lie flat, I don't think they will see you. The outcropping rises only ten feet above ground level. I'm going to hang your underpants on that little ash tree below it. They can dry there if nobody shows up. Otherwise, they will be bait."

"Bait?"

"They won't hesitate to go to the underpants, I promise."

"Then what?"

"I creep to the edge of the outcropping, look down and shoot somebody. Hopefully, they have split up. If not, we've got trouble. You stay put, whatever you do."

Several hours later, Rylee saw a flash of red in the trees far down the mountain slope, obviously someone following their trail. She recalled that the man called Tomcat wore a red shirt. She judged him a merciless, ruthless man, and Jessica had mentioned he was one of the men who abducted her at the theater. But he was alone, which seemed unlikely, and that worried her.

"Okay lady, drop your Colt, and you might live a few minutes longer. Tomcat said not to kill you unless you forced it, but I'm more than willing to squeeze the trigger."

She dropped her pistol, and it clattered on the rocks at her feet.

"Now turn around real slow-like."

She obeyed and confirmed that the gunman was the one-eyed man called Patch, a slim man of average height with a scraggly beard, not an unduly intimidating sort were it not for the six-gun in his right hand and the Winchester cradled in his left arm.

"Ain't you the pretty thing all gussied up like that." He nodded toward Jessica, crumpled up behind the rocks, apparently unconscious again. "What's wrong with your friend?"

"She's very ill."

"Well, let's see what old Tomcat wants to do about her when he gets here. Now you just step a good ten feet away from that gun of yours and set your ass down, while we wait a spell."

Chapter 24

"THIS IS THE Ghost Trail," Wolf said when they came upon the narrow, winding path that snaked upward into the higher mountains. He dismounted and made a quick study of the trail and the rocks and grass that framed it. "Plenty of use lately. Fresh horse dung. I don't know who else it could be."

The always dubious Brigham Paris said, "I don't see any sign of the cliff dwellings we're looking for."

"You won't for a half hour or better. This trail has a lot of twists and turns before the dwellings come into sight. And that's when the serious climb begins. We'll come to a flat rock shelf that extends back into a big dimple in the mountain wall for over a hundred feet. There should be a bit of grass there, and we'll see the last of the trees till we get back. No water, but as I recollect there's a stream cutting across the trail and tumbling down the mountain slope before we get there."

The deputy said, "You sound like you plan to leave the horses behind."

"I guess you're the last word on that, but I like Gabe's idea of walking it. Even in the dark, somebody's more likely to see riders coming up the trail. Besides, there's the risk of a horse's whinny or the clatter of horseshoes on rock as we get closer. Also, we can hug the wall at the narrowest spots without chancing a mount's misstep that sends us five hundred feet into the canyon below."

"You've won the argument. We leave the horses."

Wolf was glad for the deputy's acquiescence and was not sorry he might have exaggerated the danger just a bit. "We won't lose any time. We couldn't have moved the horses faster than a slow walk."

"I understand. I just ain't much for walking if I can ride."

"The distance isn't that great, but it's dang steep, and like I said before, the trail winds around so much it can make you dizzy. I'd guess a two-hour climb. After we get to the flat, we'll have about three hours before sundown. I'd recommend grabbing some naps and digging into some of the grub before we go. No fires, of course, but we have some biscuits left over from breakfast and whatever jerky we've each got left."

When the four men arrived at the wide, deep fissure in the sandstone mountain wall, Wolf was relieved to find it was as he remembered it. As the riders reined off the trail and into the large recess, they found shade beneath two towering cottonwoods that seemed out of place here and the scattering of junipers that thrived everywhere. The grass was not lush but ample enough to please staked-out horses that were ready for a rest. Pickings had been worse for critters this journey.

The men sat under the cottonwood trees as they ate their meager provisions. "We're getting short on grub," Josh said. "Maybe our friends up at the cliff dwellings will have some to spare." He turned his head toward the canyons and valley below when he thought he heard the faintest sound of gunshots. He looked at Wolf, who nodded.

"I heard it, too," Wolf said. "Three shots at least. It could have been four or five or more miles away. Gunshots echo through these mountains like thunder."

"I didn't hear anything, but I'm near deaf in one ear. Too close to a cannon during the war," Paris said.

"Yeah, somebody was shooting, but who knows what," Gabe said.

"Pistols," Wolf said. "So the shots didn't come from hunters."

Fifteen minutes later, there were more gunshots. Wolf said, "Rifle, probably a Winchester. Not a Sharps or big gun."

The deputy said, "I could hear something that time. Are you sure they're not from the cliff dwellings?"

"They're not," Wolf said. "The question is what does it mean? It's not likely a hunter out here in the middle of nowhere. I don't like this, but I suspect our answers, if any, are at the cliff dwellings." He feared what they might learn there.

Several hours later as the sun began to hide behind the mountain tops, the posse members picked up canteens and rifles to ready for their challenging hike. Wolf noted that Deputy Paris had seemingly enjoyed a nice snooze, but the mysterious gunfire had derailed his own, and he suspected that of Gabe and Josh, too. Of course, the deputy did not actually know either woman and was able to stay somewhat detached from emotional aspects of the mission, and that was not necessarily a bad thing.

The moon was a victim of cloud cover as they started the trek with Wolf in the lead. The darkness demanded extra caution along the pathway, because the footing was tricky and unknown. Wolf had traveled this way before, part of the time astride his mount, and afoot leading his horse on the more treacherous segments, but trails changed. Wind, rain and other forces of nature had a way of playing tricksters, and for all he knew a huge gap could exist in the path since the last traveler passed through. Serious problems were unlikely, he thought, since others had recently passed over the trail, however, he knew better than to take anything for granted.

Josh, who trailed him, spoke softly, "The isolation of this place is unbelievable. Perfect for defending against attacks from enemies but getting food and supplies here would be a challenge."

"The trail from the west side is wide and levels off into the mountainside. The occupants didn't have wagons, or horses for that matter, but a man could get a wagon there. That was my exit the time I visited because I was headed westward to Navajo lands. My concern is that these no-goods will try to escape that way, and, of course, since we don't have our horses with us, they'll get a day's lead on us. That's why I'm hoping we can position a man with a rifle near their remuda to cut off access."

"We could run the critters off down the west access."

"Yeah, but we'd want to hold some back for the ladies and any prisoners. For now, I'm thinking we find the women and get them away and cut them off from their horses. Now is when we could use a few more guns."

"If we can find her a rifle, Rylee can fight and shoot with the best."

"I'd forgotten that. I'm the one with Indian blood, but she's more savage than I am in the wild. And she's got no fear—maybe not enough. Her bank customers would never believe that the refined, financial wizard across the desk can cut a man's throat without blinking."

A voice came from behind them. "You fellers are making me nervous talking about Rylee like that," Gabe said.

Josh said, "You're safe if you don't cross her, but if you two marry up, you dang well better save your eyes, hands and man parts for your wife."

"I've never heard her talk about such things. I knew her folks were killed, and she was taken by Comancheros, and that Jael rescued her. That's all. She's an intelligent and refined woman."

"Yep. She is that, too."

"Changing the subject, have you two noticed that our lawman is falling behind us?"

Wolf slowed his pace and tossed a look over his shoulder before stopping. Deputy Paris was nearly a hundred feet back. "We'll wait and give us all a rest. We can't chance showing up short a man. This is a tough climb for any man, and it's a killer for a man who isn't on his feet much or carries a few extra years."

Josh said, "And the deputy's got both problems."

When Deputy Paris approached, they could hear his huffing and wheezing before he reached them. They had halted at a wider stretch on the trail, and he plopped down, leaning his back against the mountain's sheer wall.

After he caught his breath, Paris said. "Have we got far to go?"

"I'd guess we're halfway," Wolf said.

"I ain't going to get any faster, I'm holding you fellers up."

"The important thing is that we all get there. You're going to walk up here behind me after we rest a spell. We'll take it slower. Are you having any dizziness?"

"No. I just don't know if I'm up to this."

"The trail gets narrower from here. Lean toward the wall when you walk. If you feel dizzy, say so. You don't want to topple the wrong way. It's not like you're walking a tightrope, horses pass through, so there's plenty of room for a man. But you can't be too careful. That applies to all of us. I think we'd better go pretty much silent from here. When we go around the next bend in the trail, we will be able to see the cliff dwellings in daylight. Too dark now, but we all know how sound carries in these mountains."

This stretch of the trail was also steeper, and Wolf figured at this hour time likely made little difference in the outcome of their quest. He moved slowly and took rests whenever he could discern from the deputy's labored breathing that the man was approaching his limit. Finally, the trail began to widen again, and he could make out the shadowy images of some of the stone structures of the dwellings ahead. He signaled a stop.

He whispered, "Wait here. I'm going ahead to scout the place. If you hear gunfire, get up there fast. No matter what I've run into, this isn't where you want to be. I'm hoping I can get the setting of things and get back down here and tell you what we're dealing with."

Chapter 25

WOLF CREPT UP the trail and slipped sound-lessly into the ancient remnants of a once busy village. He paused and listened near the empty doorway of an empty abode. The breeze emit-ted a soft whistling, almost flutelike, sound on its jour-ney in and out of the openings in the structures. Some might call the sounds ghostlike, and he wondered if the eerie concert might have contributed to the Ghost Mesa identification.

He stepped cautiously through the stone ruins and froze when he saw the dying embers of a fire flaming briefly when the breeze struck just right and then dy-ing back to spots of glowing red. He crouched down and moved nearer and stopped again when he saw two appar-ently occupied bedrolls stretched out on the earth near the coals. Moonlight would be helpful now, he thought, and suddenly the clouds opened and admitted the moon's soft lamp. It was as if a ghost had responded. If so, at least the spirit appeared to be on his side.

Yes, there were two men, but he could see no sign of others. He heard the nickering of a horse now somewhere beyond the sleeping men and circled around them. He was soon overlooking the exit trail, and he could now see the remuda staked out and grazing on a lower level. Anyone fleeing would not retrieve and saddle his mount quickly. Wolf could not get a precise count, but he estimated there were eight to ten horses below.

But where were the riders? He made his way around the ruins and paused at one of the kivas where he smelled blood and death. He dropped to his knees and peered in. He could see a form lying at the bottom but could not tell if it was man or woman. He had to know, so he stepped onto the ladder and lowered himself into the pit-like structure.

Close-up, he could see that the body was clearly that of a man, his face mashed and bloody like someone had taken a sledgehammer to it. What in blazes was going on here? It was too dark to search the circular room, so he climbed out before he got trapped here and quietly wound his way through the ruins and returned to his comrades. He found them relieved at his appearance.

Wolf told them what he had found. "As near as I can determine, aside from the dead man, there are only two men at the cliff dwellings. There would be four unaccounted for, but I couldn't find a trace of them and no sign of Rylee and Jessica. I'm guessing that somehow they escaped, and the others are looking for them."

"That sounds like Rylee," Josh said. "She would have figured out that their chances were slim to none if they remained with these men. A death sentence had already been decided upon by someone."

"The so-called prince," Paris said.

Wolf said, "Well, let's remove these two from the picture. If we can take them alive, we might learn something." He explained where the horses were located. "Josh, I'd like you to position yourself with your rifle somewhere between the sleeping men and the horses. Among the ruins you ought to find good cover someplace. I'm hoping they don't even get an opportunity to run for it, but we don't want to chance it."

Paris said, "I want to make a formal arrest."

Of course, he would. "Fine by me. I'm hoping we can sneak up to them and take them while they're rolled up in their blankets. I can follow right behind you." He turned to Gabe and said, "Gabe, I want you to stay back and find a protected spot. Aim that Winchester at the sleeping men and be ready to fire if something goes wrong."

When they entered the ruins' site, Josh split off to circle around to his position. The other three crept toward the location of the sleeping men. Gabe removed his boots, but the deputy scoffed at Wolf's suggestion. Wolf cringed at the clatter of the rocks against the deputy's boots as they moved toward their objective. He seemed to drag one foot a bit. Even with moccasins, walking softly was a skill that a man must acquire, although he noticed that Gabe was walking almost soundlessly.

When they were within thirty feet of the sleeping men, Wolf tapped Gabe on the shoulder signaling that the young lawyer should seek his cover. Then he paused, stretching his arm out to stop the deputy. "Back away slowly."

"No, I'm going to make an arrest." Paris broke away, drawing his six-gun as he marched toward the bedrolls.

Wolf didn't bother to whisper. "Brig, get back here. Take cover. It's an ambush."

Paris stepped up to the bedrolls. "Get your asses up, gentlemen, I'm a deputy U.S. marshal, and you are under arrest." A rifle cracked from one of the cliff dwellings, and Paris tumbled forward onto the empty blankets.

Wolf dropped to the ground just as another shot was fired and tore through the air and passed over him. Then there was gunfire from behind him. Two rifles. He hoped one belonged to a posse member. Winchester clutched in one hand, he rolled behind part of an old foundation that was no more than three or four bricks high. It would provide some cover, but his vulnerability depended upon how high in the dwellings the shooter was positioned. Another shot kicking up dust just inches from his hip told him the ambusher was set up too high for comfort.

More gunfire behind him and then a groan. Gabe was firing at the ambusher in the dwellings now and drawing gunfire away from Wolf. He thought of making a dash to the fallen deputy but decided it would be suicidal until they took down the shooter. Then he saw Gabe break from the darkness, dodging behind what stone remnants he could find as he charged the dwellings that were built into the sandstone mountain wall. The gunman began firing at the young man, but this time Wolf spotted the rifle's flashes and got off several shots of his own to give Gabe some cover.

Suddenly all was quiet. Gabe had disappeared. He hoped that the young man had not been hit. Finally, the silence was broken by a whimpering, obviously from one of the shooters behind him. Then a cry. "Help me. I don't want to die. I don't want to die." Neither the voice nor pleas were Josh's, so it had to be someone who was wounded by him.

There was still no sign that they were up against more than two men. That could change, of course, but none had come out of the rocks. They needed to get to the shooter in the second tier of dwellings, and they would have the situation under control. Until then, he could kill them all. He fired another shot where he had last seen the rifle fire and received two more in exchange before the shooter's gun fell from the window-like opening and landed on the ground below.

Gabe stuck his head out, "All clear. I'll try to drag this guy down to you. The entry's more slide than stairs any-how."

Somehow Gabe had found an entry and climbed to the outlaw's nest, taken him down without firing a shot. The kid obviously had more grit and cunning than he had judged. Sometimes the quiet ones would surprise a man. Confident that any threats had been aborted for the moment, Wolf got up and headed for Brigham Paris who was sprawled motionless and facedown across the outlaws' bedrolls.

When he reached the deputy and knelt beside him, he was still uncertain whether the man lived. The darkness veiled any breathing, but when he placed his hand on the man's back, he felt the rise and fall that signaled life. He traced his fingers over Paris's back until sticky blood bonded them together like glue. The right lower back of the shirt was blood soaked, and with a bit of probing Wolf found the hole in the fabric that revealed the location of the entry wound.

He grasped the deputy's shoulder and shook it gently. "Brig, it's Oliver Wolf, can you hear me?"

A muffled voice replied, "Damn right. I didn't know who you was. Had my six-gun under the blanket, ready to use it if you was the wrong guy."

"I don't know the man's condition, but he's done with his shooting. You've got a back wound. I can't tell how bad it is."

"I sure as hell know I got a back wound, but I can move my feet and legs, so that's good, ain't it?"

"I'd say so. I'd like to get a better look, but we need to get the fire built up. You're in a good spot right now, so I don't favor moving you. Can you hold out right here a spell?"

"Don't look like I got much choice."

"I'll be back shortly and get us a fire going and then we'll tend to you as best we can."

"I arrested a pile of blankets. That's a hell of a thought."

"You're alive to laugh about it."

"Ain't nothing to laugh about."

Wolf headed in the direction where he last saw Josh, but almost bumped into him when he stepped out from the ruins. "Startled me. I was looking for you but didn't know where you ended up."

Josh said, "I was waiting to see who you were. There was a lot of shooting over this way."

"That's over. Gabe got the guy who was playing sniper. The young man's alright in a gunfight."

"I could have told you that. As they say, Gabe's a good man to ride the river with. Because he's on the quiet side some tend to underestimate him. He uses that to his advantage in the legal business."

"Well, Paris took a back shot, but he's alert and sassy. We've got to build up the fire so we can look at the wound. If you want to talk to him and see what you can do about the fire, I wouldn't complain. I'll try to find Gabe and his prisoner."

"You two are like a couple of dogs fighting over the same bone. Yeah, I'll tend to Paris. You go ahead."

"You were having a showdown with somebody. You don't seem the worse for it."

"I'm sorry to say he's dead. Younger guy, maybe not as old as Gabe. Doesn't make me feel good, but he was aiming to be part of the ambush."

"Then you probably saved my skin. I owe you."

"You owe me nothing. I'm way behind if we were keeping score."

Chapter 26

WOLF FOUND GABE dragging a man from the cliff dwellings by his feet. His prisoner had evidently been unconscious and was starting to resist when the Cherokee came upon them. Gabe stopped when he saw Wolf and dropped the man's feet, tugging his rifle out from its precarious position under his arm.

"Looks like you caught a live one," Wolf said.

"Yeah, while he was shooting at you, I slipped up and bashed his head with my rifle butt. He dropped like a sack of flour, but he's starting to wake up now."

"The other one's dead, I'm hoping this one will be willing to talk, so we can find out what happened to the women."

"What about the deputy? I saw him go down."

"He's wounded but talking. Josh is looking after him right now." He filled Gabe in on the details while they each took a leg and drug Hackler over the rock-strewn ground to the vacated bedrolls. He started to curse and squirm as they pulled him, so Wolf figured he was doing fine.

When they got there, Wolf was glad to see that Josh was already building up the fire and that an ample supply of firewood had been stacked by the outlaws. They needed the light to examine Paris' wound, but it had turned cold, and the heat generated would be welcome, too.

They propped the prisoner, who was able to sit now, against a log that had evidently been moved in from the lower level to serve as a campfire bench. "Watch him while I check on the deputy. Then we'll have a chat with the man," Wolf told Gabe.

He joined Josh at Paris's side and saw that Josh had already rolled the shirttails up to reveal the wound. He perused the entry and noted that the lead slug had burrowed without tearing the outer flesh. He probed around the area, and Paris groaned.

Wolf said, "I can't feel the slug, so it's buried deep. From the location, it appears it's in muscle. Likely won't kill him unless it putrefies, but that's a risk even if we cut it out. I'm thinking we should get him to a doctor and let the doc cut it out—or leave it if he thinks that's best. What do you think, Josh?"

"Yeah, that's what I thought. I can cut some strips of cloth off the dead man's shirt to wrap it. I think I've got some gauze in my saddle bags I can make a compress of, and a clean handkerchief we can use for now."

Paris said, "I sure as hell don't want no Injun cutting on me."

"If I did, I'd scalp you while I was at it," Wolf said.

Josh said, "I'll do what I can with the wound. Doctor Micah Rand in Santa Fe was an army surgeon. He's the best for gunshot wounds. He'll know what to do."

"I just want to get off my belly," Paris said.

"As soon as I get the wound wrapped, we'll see what you can do."

Wolf moved to the prisoner. The man appeared fully conscious now, but he was obviously in pain. A quick look at his skull revealed a serious gash and swelling that was likely just getting started. He called to Josh who was walking to the body to retrieve cloth for bindings. "I've got a man here who can use some of those bandages, so get plenty."

He sat down on the ground in front of the outlaw. "We're going to have us a talk. You can lie if you choose, but that will guarantee a hangman's noose. You just shot a deputy U.S. marshal. You'd better be praying he lives."

"Didn't know he was a marshal. Thought you was outlaws sneaking up on us. Richie was up taking a piss, and he heard rocks rattling back toward the trail."

"What's your name?"

The outlaw hesitated. "Hackler. They call me Hack. There ain't no paper out on me. Never so much as been in jail for drinking and brawling."

"You never got caught. We know you robbed the bank in Santa Fe and that you abducted two women. You can waste time denying it, but if we find those women dead, they'll hang the lot of you. But I doubt if you'd even get as far as the Santa Fe gallows."

"I can lead you to who's masterminding all of this. What's that worth?"

"I can't guarantee anything. The deputy might when he's in condition to talk. I want to know about the women. I know they were here. I found the dead man in the Kiva." He did not add that he had not found trace of Rylee O'Brian and Jessica Chandler there.

"That was Jackson. They kilt him. Mashed his head with one of them old bricks. They got away."

Wolf looked up at Gabe who was still standing by with a rifle pointed at Hackler's head. Gabe nodded and surrendered a small smile.

Wolf said, "And your other men are trying to chase them down?"

"Yeah. They broke off into two pairs. I ain't heard back, but expect they'll bring the ladies back soon. This would be the second night out for the men. They waited till dawn after the night that the women left. At least one of them women had a gun hid out. Jackson was shot with a small caliber—likely a derringer—before they hammered his brains out. They took his Colt and gun belt with them."

"That would be Rylee," Wolf said.

"Not the Rylee I know," Gabe said.

"Well, I guess you're learning about another side of the young lady. I suspect that you have a few surprises for her, too."

"What do you mean?"

"Most folks have many sides to them. My life with Tabby is an adventure. It seems every day I learn something new about her. Keeps life interesting."

"Yeah, I guess I can see that. Riding the trail out here with you, I'd never figure you for an artist. I suppose you've got lots of surprises hidden away."

"More than a few I'd just as soon keep buried. Now back to our friend here."

He studied Hackler's face illuminated by the flames briefly before they darted away with the wind and left it in the shadows. How much of what the man said was believable? It didn't matter, he thought. Whatever truths he could sort out, would be more than they knew before. "Tell me about the men who are looking for the women."

Hackler said, "I don't know much to tell. Tomcat and Patch paired off. As you might guess, Patch is a one-eyed feller. I ain't knowed him long. Does what he's told without a fuss. Tomcat would be the leader of the two. Cocky bastard. Always after the women—suppose that's how he got his moniker. Big, quick-tempered fella, but tends to fight more with his mouth than his fists."

"The others?"

"That'd be Moose and Marco. Moose is a big, tall fella with chin whiskers and a big nose. Good man in a gun fight, the best of the bunch, I'd say. Marco's a short, sturdy man. Walks with a limp. Him and Moose are good friends. They won't be moving as fast because of Marco's gimpy leg, but the two work together good and add up to more brains than the other pair."

"Did you hear gunfire to the south late afternoon?"

"I didn't hear nothing."

Wolf assumed the man was lying, but it did not matter. The other men weren't here, so it seemed safe to assume they were engaged in a search as Hackler admitted and that there had been an encounter of some kind. He feared that did not bode well for Rylee and Jessica.

He spent another ten minutes with Hackler, but the man was becoming less cooperative as he recovered from the head blow. He looked at the ugly head wound again, deciding that it could wait a bit before binding. He turned to Gabe. "Can you watch this guy while I talk to Josh and Paris?"

"Yeah, I hope he tries something. But one thing."

"What's that?"

"I'm going with you. I know what you're up to."

Wolf gave a wry smile. "Yeah. I suppose you do. I'll count you in."

When he joined the others by the fire, he saw that Josh was almost finished wrapping the deputy's wound. He had tied his rags together and taken several rounds about the lower back and looped another down to the inner thigh and back as an anchor to keep the back-wrapping from slipping upward.

"You should have been a doc," Wolf said.

"Nah. This is my limit. I don't have the patience for the cutting. Did you learn much over there?"

"Nothing we couldn't have figured out. We need to get him back to Santa Fe alive if we can. He claims to know things he's willing to bargain with. That's your territory, Brig."

Josh said, "So what happens tomorrow?"

"Brig needs to get to a doctor. Can you ride, Brig?"

"Guess I'll have to. Tie me on if I'm having trouble."

"I'm thinking you two would head back with the prisoner and the horses. To get Brig out of here, you would pick one of the outlaw's critters. You'd still need to walk a few short stretches. Turn the other horses loose. I wouldn't be surprised if a few tagged along after you. Take all our mounts with you. Gabe and I won't be coming back this way."

Josh said, "I'm thinking we'll head for Slash R. It shouldn't be more than two days and one night's ride from here. My dad will loan us a buckboard and team and an extra man. We'd spend a night at the ranch and get a few decent meals and some rest. There are decent wagon roads from the Slash R to Taos and then to Santa Fe, another three nights, I suppose. But you will be left without horses."

"We'll find our way home eventually, likely the same way Rylee's already figured out. The only direction they could have gone in these mountains is south. I'd look for the Rio Chama if I was her."

"Do you really think they're alive?" Josh said.

"Can't say. Odds are no better than fifty-fifty, but we've got to find them. If things went the wrong way, we should either bring the bodies home or see them buried."

Josh's eyes teared up. "They've got to be alive. If not, I hope you'll see every one of those men dead before you start back. The gallows can take care of Hackler."

"Don't forget the man who ordered it all," Paris said. "That's who I came to Santa Fe to get."

Wolf said, "We all need rest. I did learn that all the saddles and tack along with bedrolls and saddlebags are stored in that end dwelling to the west. I'm going to find some rope or cut some reins off to bind Hackler's wrists and ankles. We can scratch up some food and other supplies in the morning. We'll help ourselves to some blankets. We'd better catch some shuteye while we can. We've got some long days ahead."

Chapter 27

RYLEE WONDERED IF the actress in Jessica had taken over as her half-naked companion lay behind the rocks moaning. When the outlaw Patch first slipped up behind them, she had appeared unconscious, but now she was stirring and seductively swaying her bare buttocks.

Patch inched nearer to Jessica, his single eye focused on her while trying to keep his six-gun pointed at Rylee. He stretched his neck to peer over the stones for a better view just before the crack of the gunshot that drove a chunk of lead into his chest. Jessica's derringer. Rylee dived for her own gun, grabbed it, and rolled over as she readied it to fire. Patch had not gone down and was moving toward Jessica now with his weapon aimed at the woman who shot him. Rylee squeezed the trigger of her

Colt twice before the man toppled over the stones that had shielded Jessica and pinned her down.

Rylee leaped to her feet and snatched up Patch's Winchester. She dropped to her belly again and crawled to the overhang to see if she could find Tomcat. At first, she feared he had disappeared and was stalking them now that he would roughly know their location, but then she caught sight of him crouched behind a big pine no more than fifty yards distant, likely awaiting a signal from his partner.

She decided to keep him guessing for a time. She turned to check on Jessica, who had crawled out from under the dead man. She nodded approvingly at her friend and pressed a finger to her lips to signal silence and lowered her hand to inform her to stay down. Jessica picked up Patch's pistol, obviously uncertain how to handle the thing. Later, Rylee would try to teach her a few things about the weapon. A person did not need to know a lot to hit a near target like Jessica had with the derringer. They had no more cartridges for the derringer, and it could be useful for her companion to have the ability to fire the six-gun.

But they must deal with Tomcat first. She checked the rifle to confirm it was loaded and levered a cartridge into the chamber. She lay on the ground with the burning sun roasting the mostly uncovered parts of her body. It felt like hours had passed, but she supposed it had not been more than thirty minutes when Tomcat's voice broke the silence.

"Patch. Are you up there?" Tomcat hollered. "You don't get them bitches to your own self."

She gave no response, suspecting that, like his namesake, Tomcat's curiosity would get the best of him. Her suspicion proved accurate minutes later when Tomcat renewed his ascent up the slope. He was not a graceful man and fell twice as he dodged from tree to tree. Rylee was confident she could have nailed him with a bullet both times, but a miss would have sent him into hiding. She figured if they remained quiet, he would soon be near enough for a sure, easy shot.

He stopped to rest a spell behind a tree and called out again. "Patch. Patch. Damn you, answer me."

Rylee whispered to Jessica, "Scream, Jess, scream."

Jessica smiled for the first time, nodded and began screaming hysterically. Tomcat stepped out and charged up the slope, not more than fifty feet from the outcropping now. Rylee stood and aimed the Winchester. "Good morning, Tomcat."

The man froze for an instant, staring at her in disbelief. He started to raise his own rifle, but her slug tore into the flesh and bone above his left eye before he completed the task and pitched backward onto the rocky slope.

Chapter 28

RYLEE AND JESSICA stripped the dead men's clothing and salvaged as much as they could wear or carry. Long-legged Rylee claimed Tomcat's britches and sheathed skinning knife, and Jessica took Patch's trousers which required no adjustment but another punched hole in the belt. Rylee was forced to roll up the pantlegs some and adjust the belt, but the britches still drooped on her like gunny sacks. Regardless, the women acquired protection from the forest's brambles and additional warmth at night.

Rylee cut the shafts and pull straps from the boots, which neither could wear with comfort, planning to fashion new sandals when they stopped for the night. The birch bark was on the verge of shredding, and she figured she could come up with more comfort and durability with the leather.

When they were ready to depart, Rylee was wearing a deerskin vest over a wool shirt with tails that fell over her buttocks and covered most of her thighs. She had an extra holstered gun belt tossed over her shoulder. Each now carried a canteen and wore wide-brimmed hats that dropped to just above their eyes. Jessica's shirt was a bit bloodied and displayed small tears where bullet slugs had ripped through, but she had chosen the smaller shirt because of a better fit. Rylee could not care less about the appearance of their attire, but she was encouraged that Jessica was showing signs of caring about such things again.

Jessica wore a holstered pistol over her hips now and carried a sheathed knife, and each cradled a rifle in one arm. They had also collected a few gold coins, which Rylee surrendered to Jessica for the theater's work. She had hoped for more foodstuffs, but seven jerky sticks were the extent of edible bounty.

"Can you walk for a few hours?" Rylee asked. "We've got a lot of daylight left, and I would like to put a little distance between us and the bodies. I'm certain there are others searching for us, and it won't be long before buzzards start circling and attracting attention. I'm not going to try to bury these men without a shovel, and I don't think we should risk more time here."

"I'll try. I don't know how far I can carry all this."

"You tell me when it gets to be too much. We may be forced to shed some of it. I can probably handle another item or two. Follow me. Say something if I'm going too fast. Don't worry. You won't be left behind."

An hour later, Rylee thought they might have traveled as far as a mile. At this rate, they would return to Santa Fe next winter. She had maintained a slow but steady pace, resting frequently, hoping Jessica could keep moving, but her companion was struggling, although so far uncomplaining and showing a bit more toughness than when they commenced their journey.

They rested right now at the crest of a lower hilltop, and Rylee studied the seemingly endless mountains, canyons and forest spread out below. She did not want to climb into the higher mountains. The upslope climbs ate up time and strength and eventually they headed downward. If they could only travel as the crow flew, she suspected they would reach the Rio Chama in little more than two days. Up and down left hikers walking in place. She noted that this hilltop, after a short walk downslope, connected with another, and there seemed to be a chain of such hills that formed a spiny ridge below the high mountain country. It angled southwest and kept the pursued to more defensible high ground.

Her route chosen, she turned to Jessica. "Can you go a bit longer? I think I have found a route that will have shorter uphill climbs that won't be nearly as steep."

"I don't know, but I'll do my best to keep up with you."

"I realize you need rest. I just want to find a good spot to settle in for the night, someplace where we can fort up some and have a good view of the surroundings. Now, let me take your gun-belt and relieve you of a few pounds, the rifle, too."

"But you're already loaded like a pack mule."

"I'm doing fine. I just want you to stay on your feet."

"I know I'm not doing my part, but I'm trying like hell to do better."

"You saved my life earlier today. I think you've done your part. Let's just keep helping each other, and we'll get home soon."

"Do you really believe that?"

"In my mind, there is no other alternative that I want to think about."

"We never got to know each other very well, but you are nothing like I pictured you. I always thought of you as sort of a mousy bank clerk who never ventured outdoors or turned her head away from numbers in a book. But out in the wild, you turn into a half-savage."

Rylee laughed, "We don't ever really know people, do we? And we're always changing, discovering things about ourselves that we didn't know were buried deep in our souls. Did you think you could kill a man?"

Jessica got to her feet. "Never thought about it, I guess, but I can't say that under the circumstances I was especially bothered by it."

"See. Maybe there's a cold-blooded killer hidden in there."

"Let's find a nest. I just want to sleep. I could stand to eat, too, and I don't think a few bites of jerky will satisfy my appetite."

They started walking again, Rylee trying to subdue the faster pace she kept wanting to pursue. They stayed as high in the ridge as they could without moving out of the trees that offered cover. She stopped when she noticed Jessica limping slightly. "Your foot's hurting."

"My right sandal fell apart, and I stepped on a stone. My instep. It's not cut, just sore."

"I've found our home for the night. We'll get you off your feet. I'll make new sandals out of the leather I salvaged from the boots before we head out tomorrow." The foot would worsen if they continued.

The location was not ideal, but she had spotted a small clearing about fifty feet downslope with several large fallen trees along the edge that might be used as the foundation for another crude shelter or defensive barriers. They would be forced to settle for the surrounding aspen and juniper as windbreaks. The fugitives would be on the southeast side of the mountain slope, which might help since any winds would likely come from the northwest.

Best of all, she saw prospects for food in the area. Several large currant bushes with ripening berries were just off their path, and where there was one, there were likely to be a good number of others scattered about. Also, she had been observing blooming stonecrop plants, some with yellow flowers, some white, growing abundantly where they might root in soil between the stones and trees wherever they might grab occasional sunlight. Jael had told her that the Comanche ate the entire plant including flowers as something of a delicacy and she learned only recently that white folks enjoyed the leaves and stems in a salad. Some raised the plants in flower gardens under an increasingly common name, "sedum."

Stonecrop, red currants, and beef jerky. They would feast tonight, although she doubted Jessica would consider it a gourmet meal. She hoped that within another few days she would be able to hunt and start a fire with the matches she had found in Tomcat's trouser pockets. She had discarded the cigarette makings they were likely intended for, but the matches were like gold. Her success at starting a fire with flint and steel was based more upon luck than skill.

She led Jessica to the campsite she had located, and her friend immediately dropped to the ground, leaning back against one of the fallen trees, a huge cottonwood, the only one of its kind she had seen this high in the mountains. Near its base, the tree was at least three feet diameter, she guessed, high enough for them to build a lean-to of branches to help defend against the chill that would descend soon after sundown. Charred upper branches on the tree suggested that it may have been struck by lightning some years back.

"You rest," Rylee said, "but I want your hat."

Jessica removed her hat and extended it to Rylee. "Just curious. Why do you need my hat?"

"I'm going to gather supper in our hats. Tonight's menu includes one jerky strip, stonecrop salad and fresh berries," Rylee announced like a waitress in a restaurant.

"I'm sorry, my sense of humor died several hours ago, and your salad sounds a bit scary."

"Maybe I'll find something else. Most beetles are quite edible without cooking." She knew her remark was not kind, but Jessica was trying her patience again. They should be thankful both were alive.

When she returned to camp with her harvest of berries and stonecrop, Jessica was asleep and turned downright hostile when Rylee tried to waken her. "I'm not hungry. I just want to sleep."

Rylee shrugged and sat down and ate her share. The stonecrop had a peppery taste and was somewhat on the bitter side, and the berries were rather tart, but they provided nourishment, and they must eat to maintain their strength. If Jessica did not eat tonight, Rylee vowed that she would in the morning or there would be a showdown. She sighed and decided she had better start working on the sleeping quarters.

Chapter 29

GABE WAS INTRIGUED by the way Oliver Wolf read sign and crafted a narrative of what had taken place as they weaved their ways through trees and undergrowth. It was midafternoon, and he sensed that they were gaining on the hunters and the prey rapidly.

Earlier, they had paused at remnants of a crude shelter someone had tried to disperse, presumably with the notion of wiping out traces of their stay. Even he, though, could see that the women had stayed here, and the imprint of boot heels said that two of the men had found the site.

Gabe said, "Two of the men are on Jessica and Rylee's trail."

"Yes, but they are not experienced trackers. They almost seem to be wandering aimlessly back and forth.

We've crossed their paths three or four times. The women stayed here the night after they escaped.

"Can you tell when the men were here?"

"The tracks aren't fresh. I can't even estimate hours, but it was much later. I don't think there is much chance the women are outrunning them. One has been having great difficulty from the beginning. Her gait is very deliberate and slow, frequent stops. Sometimes one foot appears to be dragging."

"That would be Jessica," Gabe said. "I couldn't keep up with Rylee in these mountains. I've hiked with her before. She's like a dang mountain goat. They'd never catch her if she was on her own."

"From what I'm seeing, I would not argue that. These men are the ones that worry me for now. They might not be experienced trackers, but the one woman you suggest is Jessica is leaving plenty of sign with all her struggle and many stops. I would bet these two were involved in the gunfire we heard."

Wolf's remark did not offer any comfort to Gabe. They would likely learn the outcome soon, and his stomach churned at the thought that he might have made this journey to recover the remains of the woman he loved. He was not certain he could deal with finding Rylee's body, probably nearly destroyed by the countless scavengers by now. He was not much of a praying man, but he recited a silent prayer now.

The two men continued following the trail that Gabe figured a child could follow now, but when darkness dropped its curtain over the mountains, they finally stopped for the night. Grateful for the blankets they had confiscated from the outlaws' bedrolls at the cliff dwellings, they set up a cold camp at a gap in the forest. The location offered a clearing no more than ten feet in diameter, Wolf pointing out that it would be difficult for any unwelcome guests to pick them out in the trees.

They gnawed on some beef jerky and ate a few slices of stale bread and then Gabe agreed to take the first of a two-hour shift for guard duty. The odds of a surprise attack were slim, but Wolf suggested they should be listening for any human voices or cries that might signal how near they were to the women or their pursuers. All that Gabe heard during his shifts were the grunts, growls and brush rustlings of nocturnal animals passing nearby, all of which chose to give the forest invaders ample space.

He noted that Wolf slept soundly when not on duty, but, as for himself, he thought he might as well have taken on the entire night's sentry responsibility. Any sleep visited only briefly because he was obsessed with the thought that Rylee was dead.

The next morning, they were on the trail with sunrise. After the usual bone-chilling night, a clear day and full sun was bringing a complete turnaround to oven-like heat.

Midmorning, when they moved higher up and away from the forest's shady canopy, Wolf signaled a halt and pointed skyward to the southwest. So many black vultures that Gabe could not count them circled, seemingly taking turns dropping from the azure sky to the earth. He swallowed hard, and momentary weakness swept over him.

Wolf said, "It could be anything. Deer, raccoon, any wild creature."

"But you don't really think so, do you?"

Wolf hesitated a moment. "No. But we can find out in about fifteen minutes."

They picked up the pace now, and soon they reached the feast, where vultures were thick on the ground, some on top of a stone outcropping and others further downslope. The lower gathering was just off the trail, so they veered in that direction, the birds scattering and many launching skyward as they approached. Gabe could make out a mass of raw, ragged flesh and bones ahead, and again he was sickened by the thought of what they might discover.

"It's a man. Too big for a woman," Wolf said.

Gabe felt an instant wave of relief, but he was not confident until they reached the ghastly remains. There was little left. By the end of the day, the bones would be picked clean. The corpse had no eyes or genitals, and most of the flesh had been ripped away, but yes, the body was too large, and the remnants of a thick, brushy mustache below where there had once been a nose confirmed the sex. Splotches of hair that did not belong to either woman stuck to the scalp also, and now he spotted hair on some of the clinging leg flesh.

Wolf said, "No boots or clothes of any kind here except a torn-up pair of undershorts in the grass. No gun or rifle. This man was stripped of everything."

Gabe turned away and hurried up the slope that led to the outcropping, less fearful now about what he might discover, yet unable to wait any longer for confirmation. Again, most of the vultures retreated when he came over the rise, but several of the more determined ones did not fly away and instead backed off into the brush.

Instantly, Gabe found his answer. The scalp of a balding man had been barely touched and provided his answer. An eye patch drooped over the side of the man's head half covering the torn flesh where his ear had been torn off. He could not tell which eye might have been missing since both sockets were empty and mangled now. None of it mattered. The two women had left the confrontation alive.

"Appears this fella took at least a couple of shots." It was Wolf, who had quietly moved up behind him. "I'm sure the other man was shot down, too, but the buzzards had stripped any trace of entry wounds. Again, they took the clothes and didn't leave any weapons behind. I found boot heels and soles, but most everything else was cut off and taken. I'm guessing they're going to make something to cover their feet. They're likely wearing some men's britches and shirts now, even the hats."

"Well, we saw their shoes and dresses at the cliff dwellings, and you said they were barefoot at the beginning and then got some birchbark for their feet. At least they aren't near naked anymore."

"Nope. I'm not sure you know this Rylee O'Brian quite as good as you thought. She's sure as hell not a helpless, little mouse."

"Well, I never saw her as a helpless person, but I didn't have a clue she was half savage, no offense intended."

"None taken. Anyhow, it appears Patch and Tomcat are no longer a threat. That leaves the two Hackler called Moose and Marco. They could have given up and turned back by now. If they find the women, they might be sorry."

"We can't be sure of that."

"No, we can't, and either way, we've got to find the women. They likely wouldn't turn down some help getting out these mountains."

"The bodies?"

"They're being cleaned up just fine, it appears to me. We'd best be on our way."

Chapter 30

RYLEE WAS RELIEVED that the more positive Jessica crawled out of their low lean-to shelter this morning. She did not think that her partner had awakened during the night, and once Rylee dropped off, she captured a good five hours dead sleep, which energized her but was dangerous in their situation.

When Jessica returned after stumbling into the woods to pee, Rylee announced, "This morning, we both eat, and you are taking a larger helping because you didn't eat last night. Your currant berries and stonecrop are in your hat, and my share is in mine. We will both clean our breakfast bowls."

"Spare me your humor at this hour of the morning."

"You will get more of it if you don't eat and maybe some anger with it." Rylee sat down cross-legged on the ground with her hat in her lap and commenced eating.

Jessica joined her, and they ate in silence except for her occasional coughing and gagging. When she finished, she said, "I can't wait for lunch."

When they headed out and moved to higher ground again, Rylee looked out over the slopes and hills below, searching for any sign they were still being followed. She tensed when she saw two figures climbing the steep slope as they exited a canyon to the northwest. They had not picked up their quarries' trail yet, because they were moving in from a direction the women had not traveled, but if they came over the crest and stayed with the ridge, it would only be a matter of time.

She was confident she could outrun them and break a lead that would force them to give up the chase, but at Jessica's pace, the men had a good chance of closing the gap. It would be a good hour's rugged walk to the crest, and if they picked up the trail, possibly another hour or two to close the gap. They had some time, but not much at their present pace. They should keep their eyes open for a hiding place or a strategic spot to defend.

If only she could find a decent sniper's perch. She and Jael spent hours target shooting, and sometimes Tabby Rivers joined them. Of course, Tabby was rarely defeated in a match, but she and Jael enjoyed pressing her. The last time women had been allowed in a holiday shooting match in Santa Fe, Tabby had claimed first place with Jael and Rylee at second and third, respectively. After that occasion the town fathers declared such matches for "men only." Since women did not have the vote, there was little political risk in such a pronouncement.

"What is it?" Jessica said.

Her mind had wandered, and she almost forgot Jessica's presence. "There are two more men down there." She pointed to where the men were moving, barely larger than ants from their position. "We had better stay to the east side of the crest. I wasn't thinking. If we can see them, they can see us if they look at the right place at the right time, which would be the wrong place and time for us."

They moved downslope not more than fifteen feet. "What are we going to do?" Jessica asked.

"Coming from that direction, there is no chance they have found our trail yet, but if they come over the top of the ridge, they'll have an opportunity open up. We need to find a place where we can hide or defend ourselves if they do come after us."

"But we won't know till they get here."

"We've got some time. We'll figure something out. Now, let's get moving."

They moved at a decent pace for almost an hour before Jessica started to wear down again. Several times she just stopped, dropped on the ground and said she couldn't go any farther. Then with a drink from the canteen, a fifteen-minute rest and Rylee's nagging, she would force herself up and walk a short spell before needing rest again.

Rylee knew it was futile to push Jessica much farther. The thought agitated her at first but then she reminded herself that her companion was a woman in her forties who engaged in very little physical activity beyond a block's walk from the Exchange apartment to the theater and back several times daily. Besides, Jessica had just lost a baby and been through more than a week of hell. That experience, with the loss of blood and resulting fatigue, would have been enough to take down most women for at least a few days, she supposed.

She caught sight of a drop-off on a slope below where the surface was ragged and loose stones were strewn about. She suspected that in years past earth and stones had pulled away and tumbled down the mountainside in a small landslide.

"Wait here, Jess," she said before stepping carefully down the steep slope to inspect the site.

It was far from perfect, but she had not seen anything more promising. The direct drop from the top would be twenty feet or more, and the concave wall that remained was not quite a cave. The recession, however, went deep enough to shelter against an attack from above and most of both sides. Descent would require Rylee's strategy of moving down the slope and circling back to approach from the front. If she could roll some of the stray rocks and boulders to the front, she could fortify the location some.

The negative was that there would be no retreat from this place. They could get pinned down here with no escape route, but she figured it did not matter because Jessica could move only at a snail's pace and would collapse in less than an hour on the run. Her hope was that they might hide out here and go undetected. It was past time for a change of luck.

She trudged back up the slope to retrieve Jessica who was sitting on the ground when she arrived, her head slumped over and dozing. "Jess, I've found us a passable hideout, but you've got to move downslope. We won't even consider moving till tomorrow afternoon, so you can sleep the next twenty-four hours if it suits you." She did not add that sleep could be interrupted in an instant. If the men had picked up their trail, they could show up at any time.

Rylee took all the weapons and canteen Jessica had been carrying and instructed Jessica to place a hand on her shoulder as they stepped down the slope. Because of steepness and a considerable amount of shale, the footing was tricky, but they were almost to their hideaway when a rifle shot cracked, and a slug kicked up stone splinters at their feet. Rylee tossed Jessica's guns and the canteens downslope, pushed Jessica to the ground. "Roll if you must. You are almost there. To your right."

Two more shots rang out, and one chipped bark on a nearby tree. She wheeled, and although she could not see a shooter, Rylee fired off two wild shots of her own to force them to slow their assault. She looked over her shoulder and saw that Jessica had angled to her left to get below the shelter and was moving the short distance back upslope to the little ridge that edged the hollow that was to have been their hideout.

Fortunately, during an apparent surge of energy, Jessica had picked up the discarded weapons and canteens. Sometimes, Jess had more good sense and grit than she gave her credit for. She just never knew which Jessica was going to turn up at a given moment.

She turned back and headed down the slope to join her comrade when a barrage of rifle fire commenced again. She was almost to the hollow and out of the shooters' sight when she felt the slug drive into the back of her thigh. Her leg buckled and she almost went down, but she regained her footing and kept on moving. She thought she was out of their sight and only now became aware of the searing pain and throbbing in her thigh.

She stumbled into the concave shelter and dropped to the floor. "I'm hit. The wound is bleeding badly. I need your help, and we've got to move fast. Those men will be here within a half hour. They'll move slower since they know we're armed, but they'll be here as sure as hell."

Jessica said, "Tell me what to do. I can take care of it."

"Cut off my left pantleg. I can tell it's already blood soaked high up. Then slice strips for a tourniquet and binding the wound." Rylee gave step by step instructions, glad that Jessica had collected herself for the moment. As soon as the wound was bound, she grabbed her rifle and, belly down, crawled to a position that offered a few stones as a barrier.

She scrutinized the slope below her and off to both sides of the hollow, but her vision suddenly blurred, and she felt weak. The blood loss. She fought off the dizziness, but she was struggling. "Jess, I'm having some problems. Get your pistol and keep an eye out. If you see anybody, squeeze off a shot. They won't move in so fast. I just need to rest for..." Her head dropped and blackness consumed her, and the rifle clattered on the shale surface.

Chapter 31

GABE LOOKED AT Wolf when he heard the gunshots. "How far away do you think?"

"Hard to say up here. Sound here carries forever it seems sometimes. Could be a couple of miles."

"I don't think so."

"Neither do I. Let's move to the crest. It appears that's where Rylee and Jessica were headed. We'll pick up their trail again from there and have a better look at the country."

Before they reached the top, they heard more gunshots and then eerie quiet took over. At the crest, they picked up the women's tracks and followed them, discovering two pair of boot tracks intersecting and trailing even as the fugitives moved downslope some.

Gabe said, "It's obvious that Moose and Marco came up from the other side and are following the women. One man's foot drags some. That would be Marco. Hackler said he walks with a limp."

"Not bad. You're about ready to take up scouting for the Army."

"I think I've found a less dangerous line of work."

"This is less dangerous?"

Gabe ignored him. Now that they had got better acquainted, Wolf didn't hesitate to needle him on occasion.

Then Wolf pressed a finger to his lips and whispered. "Did you hear somebody moving through the brush ahead?"

"No, but I'll take your word for it."

"I think I'll cut off downslope and see if I can get ahead of whoever it is. You stay with the trail."

Gabe nodded. That was fine with him, because he knew he was following Rylee. When Wolf disappeared into the trees, Gabe continued the trail until he walked onto a little rise and froze, instantly dropping to his knees. He saw a tall man slinking down the slope toward a wall where part of the mountain had been carved out like a slice of cake. He inched his way in behind the man until he was not more than fifty feet distant. Then he saw the women, one holding a pistol, the other stretched out on the floor of the recess in which they were making their stand.

His heart raced upon confirmation that the one lying still was Rylee. She must have taken one or more of the slugs. He had no doubt she was wounded and fought off the thought that she might be dead. He flinched when he heard the pistol fire once and after a pause a second time. It was aimed somewhere below. She was unaware of the man creeping in from this side. Gabe suspected the stalker was the man called Moose, considering his size.

Moose had a clear shot and was readying his rifle now. Gabe leaped to his feet, shouldering his Winchester, and yelled, "Moose." The startled man turned toward the voice, giving Gabe just enough time to aim the rifle and squeeze the trigger. Moose staggered forward a few moments before he dropped his rifle and tumbled backward just as Gabe's second slug burrowed into his chest.

Gabe rushed down the incline as fast as footing would allow, but stopped when he realized pistol shots were being fired his way. "Jessica, it's Gabe Laurent. Don't shoot," he yelled.

She paused but then a rifle's crack and the sound of lead digging into a tree trunk less than a yard away reminded him of the second man. Fool. In his rush to get to Rylee, he had thrown caution to the wind. He dropped to the ground again and waited. Two shots came from

downslope, but there was no indication they were direct-
ed his way. Silence.

He waited and a few minutes later saw Wolf emerge
from the woods below. He got to his feet and continued
his original course to the escaped captives. He reached
the hollow before Wolf and was nearly knocked off his
feet when Jessica fell against him, clutching him so tightly his ribs hurt, sobbing uncontrollably. "Thank, God,"
she said. "I thought we were dead."

He wanted to get to Rylee, who lay face down in the
dirt and shale. He tried to step back and pull away, but
Jessica did not take the hint. "Rylee. Is she..."

"Shot in the thigh. We patched it. She said the tourniquet should be released when the bleeding is controlled.
So much blood I almost puked. I should let you check her,
shouldn't I?"

She finally released him, and he went to Rylee and
knelt beside her. Wolf arrived, and Jessica immediately
captured him.

First off, Gabe confirmed she was breathing. Then he
bent over and kissed the back of her neck. She moaned,
raised her head and started struggling to get up, one
hand reflexively searching for her rifle. "Rylee, it's Gabe.
Everything is alright now. The outlaws are dead."

She collapsed on her side, winced, and looked at him, her dark eyes apparently disbelieving of his presence. She replied with a soft, raspy voice. "Gabe? What are you doing here?"

"Looking for you."

"I must be asleep, and I'm dreaming."

"Jessica said you were shot and lost a lot of blood. We need to get you drinking."

"Whiskey would be nice."

She had not lost her sense of humor. She would pull through this. "Jessica said you have a thigh wound. May I look at it?"

"You're always wanting to look at my thighs. Help yourself but be gentle."

"We'll need to roll you back on your stomach."

"Something besides rocks and dirt would be nice for a bed."

"We brought blankets, but we dropped them and our canteens up the slope a ways when we decided to deal with your stalkers. We'll offer more luxury later." He helped her roll over and turned his attention to the thigh, immediately removing the tourniquet and tugging the wrapping from the wound. The bleeding was no more than an ooze now, and he figured the tourniquet should not be necessary. He probed the flesh about the entry point with his fingers. Puffy but not terribly swollen.

"Tell me what you are seeing, dang it. I don't like silence when somebody's poking around my ass."

He rolled his eyes. The sassy Rylee still endured. "Does it hurt?"

"If you can't ask better questions than that, I'm going to demand another doctor. Hell yes, it hurts, but you can't make me scream."

"Alright. I have removed the tourniquet. Not much bleeding now. I don't think the slug's buried too deep. I think I felt the slug. I'm not sure."

Wolf had escaped Jessica's aggressive embrace now and moved in beside Gabe. "What do you think?" Gabe asked.

Wolf traced his fingers over the swollen flesh and spent some time near the entry wound. "You're right. It is the slug. It will be a week, maybe two, before we can get her to a doctor. I can remove it with my knife. The blade could have some nastiness on it. We should get a fire started so I can heat it."

"I can hear you, Oliver, and you are not going to use that big butcher knife of yours to cut the slug out. I've got a penknife in my pocket, and you can use that," Rylee said.

"Glad to. That would be much better. I can remove the slug quickly, but it will be painful. I've got nothing to give you but a stick to bite on."

"I'll pretend I'm a beaver. Just do it soon."

Within an hour they had a warming fire. Gabe had retrieved the blankets and canteens, and both women were stretched out on blankets near the concave hollow wall. Another blanket covered Jessica, and she was cocooned and sleeping soundly.

Rylee, however, awaited the knife blade while Gabe held her hand with a thick juniper twig at the ready. Wolf crouched beside her positioning the hot knife blade above the wound. "I have nothing to stich this with, but I have gathered leaves of the heal-all plant and will make a poultice to cover the wound. The open wound will drain some, and that is a good thing, but it will leave a puckered scar."

"I don't care. I can't see it, and nobody else is going to see it."

"Nobody?" Gabe said.

She did not reply.

Wolf touched the entry wound with the blade, but before Gabe could press the twig between her teeth, Rylee fainted dead away. By the time she opened her eyes, the wound was bound, and she was covered with a blanket.

Gabe was returning with an armload of firewood when he saw she was awake. "Tell me when you can drink some more," he said. "I've filled the canteens with fresh spring water. You've got to keep drinking."

"It's over?"

"Yep. Oliver is out hunting. We've still got a good hour before sundown. Would you eat some venison?"

"I'd eat a horse or a dog. I just want meat."

The echo of a gunshot resounded from lower on the slope. "I think you will have venison."

"It's getting cooler. I can't believe I'll have fire and blankets tonight. This is like a hotel in the wilderness. But you and Oliver don't have blankets now."

"I was hoping you would share yours with me."

"I guess I could. It just seems strange doing that when there are others here."

"We'll have our clothes on. You're recovering from a gunshot wound. The others will be right next to us. I think your virtue is safe."

"I'm not concerned about my virtue. I'm a banker, and I don't want to be the subject of a scandal."

"And I'm a lawyer, and I don't give a dang. Besides, you're talking about Jessica Chandler and Oliver Wolf. They are the least likely gossips in Santa Fe."

"I guess you're right, and I've had enough of freezing out in these mountains."

"You could quit worrying about all this if you'd just marry me, Rylee. I've asked you a half dozen times. I love you, and you claim to love me. It's time. These past days have made me think. You never know what tomorrow brings. We should get on with life."

"She's right, dear. I think you should marry this brave man."

Gabe turned and saw Jessica stretched out on her side her head propped on her elbow. He had forgotten about her. She had been awake and listening.

Chapter 32

JOSH RIVERS WAS struck by how much his father, Levi, had aged. The lines on Levi's leathery, sun-bronzed face seemed deeper now, especially the vee crevices that ran from the corners of his eyes. He was stepping more carefully these days, not as sure-footed as he once was. He could never remember his dad's exact age, but he was several years past seventy-five. It seemed to Josh he had grown old in just the three months since father and son last visited.

Levi's stubborn streak had not faded, however, and Josh was glad that his stepmother, Dawn Rutledge Rivers, was a patient soul. Probably a dozen years younger than Levi, Dawn was the old man's anchor and quick to step in to moderate disputes between Levi and Josh's brother, Nathan, the only one of the five children to stay on the Slash R. She had been nothing short of a blessing to the family.

Josh's mother, Aurelie, had been killed in the same Comanche raid as Josh's wife and Michael's mother, Cassandra, and the then one-year-old Michael had been abducted by the raiders that day.

The two men stood a good distance from the buckboard, where Michael was waiting at the reins of a mule team and the wounded deputy marshal lay stretched out in the wagon bed. As they stood there under the shade of a towering cottonwood, Josh noticed that he now stood a few inches taller than his father who had once matched his height at two inches above six feet. The old devil had to be shrinking, because he sure as hell hadn't been growing.

"Now, don't you let that Comanche you're married to keep Michael from coming back here."

"Pop. Jael's not Comanche. She was a captive like Michael, and we can be darn thankful she was in that village to adopt him as her own."

"I like Jael good enough, but she's still got Comanche ways about her and so does the boy. Hell, a week back a couple of stray Comanches stopped by to water horses—don't know why they was off the reservation—and we invited them for dinner since it was almost noon. Danged if

Michael didn't take up with them, chattering with those fellers in Comanche like he's never left the tribe."

"That was his first language, Pop. He and Jael speak it sometimes. She doesn't want him to forget."

"But them redskins kilt your ma and your wife and took your baby son. I'd think you'd want kill the Comanche in him."

"It's a part of what he is, Pop. Another language and knowing about other people can be useful. He's fluent in Spanish, too. Jael insisted on it, and she taught him. He polished it with all the Spanish speaking folks we've got in Santa Fe. That could be very useful in this part of the country."

"Won't argue that. That ought to be about enough, I'd think. I know that woman speaks every language in the world, but a rancher don't need more than Michael's learned."

"Well, maybe he won't be a rancher."

"He's born to ranch. He loves it here, and he takes to it like a cow to tall grass. Nate's boys ain't turning out to be likely prospects. Eli's going up to Denver in the fall for more schooling. Going to live with your brother Ham and his woman. Ham won't let him come back. He'll get that kid into banking or some city business. Hell, he might even end up a dang law wrangler—like we need another in the family."

Levi never had approved of Josh's choice of professions. He was to have been a rancher, also. Nate, the eldest of the sons, had never had much choice, but he seemed happy with his lot. "What about young Levi?"

"He does ranch work because he's told to. He'd rather stay in the house and read. Smart boy, but he ain't ranching material. Nate says Katherine—she's just a few months younger than Michael—would like to be a rancher. Ain't that a hell of a thing? Two sons, and it's the daughter that wants to ranch."

"Well, Pop, we don't control those things. And I know several darn good women ranchers. Time sorts it all out. And I've got to be going. I've already said goodbye to Dawn."

"One more thing. Nate will be in about five days behind you to get the wagon stocked with supplies and ride back with Michael, but before then, you have a little chat with your son."

"What kind of chat?"

"About boy and girl cousins."

"I don't understand."

"Him and Katherine have taken to each other. Everybody's noticed. You explain to him about cousins. If you think he's ready, somebody can take him up to Cimarron and introduce him to a whorehouse there."

His father's remarks stunned him for a few moments. Finally, he said, "I'll talk with him, but I'd better not hear of anybody taking him to a bordello." He was miffed at the old man now and decided he had best get moving. "And maybe Julia should talk to Katherine. I'm sure their friendship is innocent."

"For now, anyhow. I see that young man taking over this ranch someday, and I just don't want trouble in the family."

Later, Josh rode his buckskin alongside the wagon, the bound Hackler, hands locked on the saddle horn, trailing behind him mounted on a bay gelding hitched to a lead rope. He peered over the side of the buckboard and saw Deputy U.S. Marshal Brigham Paris stretched out on a straw mattress, sleeping soundly with a blanket pulled over his shoulders.

He worried about the deputy. He was resting in luxury now compared to his days on the trail to the Slash R from the Ghost Mesa cliff dwellings, but his skin was hot now, indicating fever, and his legs seemed seriously affected by the back wound. The wounded man could barely move them, and he had to be assisted, half dragged sometimes to a place to relieve bowels and bladder. He questioned that the man should even move until examined by a physician, but Paris refused to undergo what he considered the indignity of dropping his waste in the bucket in the wagon bed.

It was slow-going this morning, winding out of the valley where the Slash R headquarters buildings were located, but they should make better time after noon. His father had assured him there should be no problem reaching Taos before sundown and that they should be able to find a few rooms at a boarding house there. Levi had added that "Michael was the best dang muleskinner on the ranch."

He was seeing his son in a new light now, wondering how he had been so blind. The boy stretched to a strong six feet now, and he might or might not be finished growing. The Rivers clan tended to early maturity and all the brothers had reached their ultimate heights early. The males were mostly on the tall side, all the brothers well over the six-foot threshold except for Hamilton, who had to wear boots to make five and a half feet. He made up for the shortfall with brains and pugnaciousness, however.

Of course, Michael would be interested in the opposite sex, but he never talked about it—in front of his parents anyway. He thought about what it was like to be fourteen going on fifteen and quickly blotted the memory out. Surely the son was a better person than his father. Jael had probably been a greater influence on the boy, since it had taken time for the boy with rust-colored hair and green-flecked brown eyes like his own to accept that a Comanche boy could have a white father. He supposed that even now Michael was closer to his adoptive mother.

That was the answer. Jael could talk to Michael about the cousin business. Did that make Josh Rivers a coward? Yep. He would broach Jael before any talk with Michael. Maybe she would take on the task. He sighed. And he also had to convince his wife to allow Michael to return to the Slash R for the entire summer.

In Taos they found main floor lodging in a boarding house operated by a Mexican man and his Pueblo wife. It had two connecting rooms, so he situated the wounded deputy and Michael in one and Hackler and himself in the other. Josh and Michael settled for their bedrolls laid out on the floor of their respective rooms, Michael not wanting to sleep with a possibly dying man, and Josh wanting to anchor the prisoner's wrists to the head-board. They enjoyed supper and breakfast at the place and were treated like royalty, the wife even trying to serve Paris in bed and seeing that a chamber pot was placed near the bed. Josh suspected that business was not good for the couple and paid them with a ten-dollar gold eagle for the one dollar per person nightly charge. The look on the woman's face was well worth it.

The next night was spent at a clearing off the well-worn trail to Santa Fe. They did not move the deputy from his mattress on the wagon. Paris was delirious now, speaking gibberish. They could get him to neither eat nor drink, and Josh started to question whether the Santa Fe destination was the undertaker or Doctor Rand.

Josh had suggested riding on through the night, but his son turned defiant. "I won't do that to the mules, Dad," Michael said. "They need rest and grazing. The horses do, too. We should break out that sack of grain in the wagon while we're at it. Six hours rest, and we can go again."

Michael was right, of course. Josh found himself proud of his son for defending the animals. After tying Hackler's wrist to a young tree and checking on the patient in the wagon bed, Josh laid out his bedroll next to the wagon and fell instantly to sleep. Later, he was awakened by his son's voice, "Don't try it, mister, or you're a dead man."

He sat up and looked around. Michael was standing not more than ten feet away, his Winchester trained on Hackler who stood above Josh with a chunk of stone in his hand. Hackler tossed the stone aside but said nothing.

Josh clambered to his feet. "What's going on here?"

Michael said, "He was going to bash your head in with that rock. I got up to go check on the critters over by the stream. I ended up staying there quite a spell. Chief needed some loving, so I spent some time with him, and when I came back, this no-good was moving toward you with the rock. Fortunately, I take my rifle whenever I step away from camp."

"Keep the gun on him till I've got him tied again." When he checked the ropes on the ground about the tree trunk, he said, "I gave this guy too much slack on the rope, thinking he might sleep better. They were loosened just enough that he could reach it with his teeth. He chewed the rope clear through, just like a danged rat."

Hackler glared. "You're a fool, Rivers. If it wasn't for this kid, you'd be dead, and I'd have your guns. That would've turned the game around."

"But you didn't get the job done, and you just dug your hole a little deeper. I'll make the marshal aware of your attempt to escape."

After the bonds were secure, Josh checked on Paris again. He didn't appear any better, but he couldn't say there had been a significant change for the worse. He built up the fire again, and he and Michael sat down in front of the crackling flames. He plucked his watch from its pocket. "Four o'clock, Michael. Past six hours by my count."

"Yeah, I'll get the mules hitched in a minute."

"I owe you, Michael. You saved my life tonight."

"You owe me nothing, Dad. You're my father. I can't repay you for the life you and Mom have given me. I know how lucky I am. It just took me a spell to figure it out."

"You've jumped from a boy to man in my head the last few days. That's not to say you know everything by a long shot. But I'm still working on that myself. It seems the more I know, the less I know. Do you know what I mean?"

"I've got to think on that. What about my going back to the Slash R till school starts?"

"You really do like the ranching, don't you?"

"Yeah, haven't you noticed how much time I spend with the horses and cattle at our place and Aunt Tabby and Uncle Oliver's."

"Yes, but I thought you were mostly having fun."

"Is there anything wrong with a man's work being fun?"

Josh thought about that. His own work was fun most of the time or he wouldn't do it. "No. We're lucky if we find that kind of work."

"Gramps hints that I might partner with Uncle Nate at the Slash R someday, and Uncle Nate and I get along fine. His boys won't stay on the ranch. Katherine might."

Oh, Lord. He was not ready for this. "I gather you get along with Katherine?"

"I do. She's the best friend I ever had. We talk about everything. I'll bet Gramps has told you about us. He has all but said that he doesn't like us being so close. He reminds me every day that we're cousins." He shrugged. "Dad, I'm years from being attached to a woman, and I know what they say about cousins pairing up. I know about sex, and I know what causes babies. I've been around animals since before I could walk. Katherine and I won't do anything dumb. I'd take it kindly if you didn't mention this little talk to Mom, though. Can't we make it a father and son thing?"

"Yeah, we can do that. We've still got to sell her on you going back to the Slash R for the summer."

"That won't be as hard as you think."

This young man would make a hell of a good lawyer, Josh thought, but you don't write scripts for somebody else's life. More often than not, such attempts ended up in the fireplace.

Chapter 33

MICHAEL REINED IN the mule team in front of U.S. Marshal Chance Calder's office. Josh dismounted and hitched his and Hackler's mounts on the rail in front, yanked Hackler off his mount, grabbed him by the shirt collar and led him through the office door.

Calder was at his desk and got to his feet when the door swung open. "Josh, what in blazes?"

"Lock this guy up. I'll explain later. I've got deputy Paris in a buckboard out front. He's in bad shape. I'm headed for Doc Rand's. Hackler here shot him, so he'd better be praying that Paris lives."

"I'll get this feller locked up and won't be far behind you."

When they reached Doctor Rand's storefront hospital, Josh asked Michael to go in and see if the doctor was available. "If he's not, ask his assistant, Camila, for a stretcher." They needed to get Paris out of the wagon and off the street.

Michael disappeared into the hospital, and Josh climbed into the wagon bed. He pressed his fingers to the forehead of the unconscious man whose breathing seemed even more labored now. The deputy's skin felt like he was on fire. It was difficult to hold out much hope for his recovery.

Michael reappeared soon with Doctor Micah Rand who was carrying a stretcher. The physician, as usual when in his office, wore a white surgical smock. With his full head of flame-red hair and a sprinkling of freckles over the nose and forehead of a boyish face, Rand appeared too young to be a physician, but Josh judged him to be several years past thirty.

Rand leaned the stretcher against the buckboard and joined Josh in the wagon. "Good afternoon, Josh. Michael told Camila this couldn't wait, so I left a patient on the examination table. Camila was going to join him and keep him company. He's a young fellow, and I really think he comes in to see her anyway. Gunshot, Michael said, back wound."

"Yeah, and he's a very sick man. He's been unconscious most of the morning. Feels like he's burning up. He can move his legs some but not much."

Rand checked Paris's pulse, pressed the back of his hand to the wounded man's cheek. "I don't need a thermometer to tell me he's got a high fever. We need to get the stretcher under him and then move him to my surgery. It's important that we support his back when we do this. Michael can take the legs and feet and you will grip him under his arms. Once we get him on the stretcher and off the wagon, we'll be fine."

In less than fifteen minutes, a limp Paris lay face down on Doctor Rand's surgery table. Rand peeled the deputy's shirt off and examined the wound. Three or four inches of swollen flesh surrounding the slug's entry wound had turned a greenish purple, and a fist-sized abscess nearly covered the wound.

Josh and Michael remained near the room's door after helping position the patient on the table. Rand looked up. "It appears that Camila and I are going to have our work cut out for us this afternoon, if you will excuse the pun. I'll have Camila come in here and stay with Deputy Paris while I finish with my other patient. We'll put a sign out and close the office for a few hours. My other appointments are not urgent, and there will be some patient complaints, but this man's life is at stake. His partial paralysis is likely caused by the swelling, incidentally, but the slug must come out, or his troubles may just be beginning."

"So you think he will live, Doc?"

Rand shrugged, "I don't know, likely won't for several days. I can do the surgery, but we have nothing very helpful to deal with infection. That will be more up to the man's body and the good Lord. We'll help all we can."

"So you don't need us anymore?"

"You've done all you can do unless you are a praying sort."

Outside, they found Marshal Calder leaning on the buggy. "Figured they didn't need another man getting in the way, but I'm sure anxious to hear about all this."

Josh turned to Michael. "Son, I'll be spending some time with the marshal. Why don't you take the buckboard and the bay and stop by the law office and see if your mother is in. She's likely wondering what became of me, and I know she'll be thrilled to see you. You can take the wagon out to the house and put up the mules and horse in the stable. Tell your mom I'll stop by the office before I go home. If she's not there, I'll see you both at our place."

"That bay gelding is a fine animal, Dad—if somebody would care for him right."

"He belonged to one of the outlaws. I'll talk to the marshal about the horse."

"I've got money saved up. I'd pay two hundred dollars for the animal."

Michael knew horses better than most traders. He was seeing something that Josh was not. "We'll see."

Chapter 34

JOSH SAT ACROSS the desk from Chance Calder in the marshal's office and told him about the posse's journey and encounter with the outlaws. A sober-faced Calder was silent for a spell when he finished.

Finally, he spoke. "So you don't know if the women are alive or dead?"

"I don't. The gunfire I mentioned doesn't encourage me, though. It will be like losing a daughter if Rylee doesn't make it. She's very special to our family. She and Jael are very close, more like sisters than mother and daughter because of their ages, I suppose."

"Does Brig Paris still think Charles Hanover is behind this?"

"Yeah. But his opinion seems to rely more upon suspicion than evidence. Our friend back there in the cell might be of some help if he would talk."

"That's what I was thinking. If he's working for Hanover, he ought to be able to tie this up for us."

"I don't think he knows that much. My impression is that another man is the link, the one who dealt directly with the gang—or gangs. Paris claims there are multiple gangs, as many as four or five working under Hanover's direction around the country."

"So we need to rope in this link and hope he will talk to save his own hide."

"I would say so."

Calder said, "I'm not sure our prisoner is so safe here, and I'm gone a lot tending to other business. I have Abe Markham who comes in late around six o'clock and stays nights, but he sleeps on the cot in the front cell most of the time. He doesn't carry a sidearm but keeps a shotgun within easy reach, but he's approaching eighty and ain't up to handling gunplay. I use Oliver Wolf sometimes, but he's wandering around in the mountains."

"Don't look at me. Do you know if my brother Cal is still in town? You mentioned seeing him."

"He was yesterday. I need to track him down. He hauled in a caravan of corpses the other day when him and Willi went to see about ransoming Rylee. We caught his interest in this case, and he just might be willing to wear a temporary deputy's badge for another stint. I think he's concerned about his wife getting after him if he doesn't get back to their ranch soon. I don't think she trusts him much. I know they've had a lot of problems."

"Yes, they got things patched up a year or so ago, and I'd hate to see things turn bad. But Cal is Cal. He couldn't resist an adventure. I think Erin worries more about Cal hitting the bottle again. I'll vouch for him if he gets into trouble at home. I think she realizes he generally uses good sense if demon rum isn't calling the shots."

"Well, I'll check with Willi to see if he knows where he might be if he's in town. Mose at the livery will know if he's left town. If you see him, send him over."

"I'll do that."

"One more thing."

"What is it?"

"If I would decide to call on the prince feller, I'm wondering if you might go with me."

"Why not Cal?"

"I wouldn't expect to use a gun that day. I think a smooth-talking law wrangler might read the situation better and maybe ask the right questions. There shouldn't be any gunplay. Cal and others would know where we went. I don't think they'd want to take on the risk of killing a U.S. marshal."

"Get word to me when you're ready. I won't be traveling anytime soon."

Chapter 35

JOSH ENTERED THE reception area of the Rivers & Sinclair offices, and without a suit and tie felt instantly out of place. He was never comfortable entering absent his office "uniform," especially during client hours. Some folks did not recognize him on the street not attired in more formal garb. Today, he was also aware that he likely carried the aroma of sweat and horseshit with him.

Linda de la Cruz was at her desk deftly racing her fingertips over the keys of her Remington typewriter. When she saw him, she paused and offered one of her warm smiles. "Welcome home, Josh. I spoke with Michael when he was in. He left just a few minutes ago. I can't believe how he's growing up and how mature he's become."

"Yes, it's also a bit scary. There's mature, and there's mature."

Her brow furrowed. "I will think on that. Not having raised any children yet, I am not certain I understand."

"You will."

"Jael will be thrilled to see you. Go on back and surprise her. She has been worried sick about you, but she won't tell you that, of course."

He headed down the hall to Jael's office, rapped softly on the door and opened it. When she saw Josh, she darted out of her chair, raced to him and fell into his arms, clutching him so tight their bodies seemed almost one. This willowy, sable-haired beauty still never failed to incite his lust, and he wished they were at home in bed.

She stepped back and said, "Welcome back, my handsome warrior. I hope you will enjoy a shave and bath before bedtime. I can help if you wish."

"You are saying I stink."

She twisted her lips and squinted one eye as if thinking. "Yes, but I love you anyway." She stepped back into his arms again, this time lifting her head to receive his lingering kiss. When they separated, Josh pondered locking the door and taking her right on the desk but remembered that the last time they tried that they tumbled off onto the floor and he ended up with a stoved-up back for a week. He doubted if he had become more agile in five years' time.

Jael took his hand and led him to the two captain's chairs on the client side of her desk, and they sat down, scooting their chairs to face each other. "Let's talk," she said. "Michael gave me a summary, but he didn't know the full story. I want to know about Rylee."

"Love, I don't know much more about Rylee than you do. I'm sure Michael told you that she and Jessica escaped from the abductors. They were holed up at a place called the Ghost Mesa cliff dwellings. Just before we arrived, we heard gunshots from the surrounding mountains in the only direction they could have gone. When we reached the hideout, I shot and killed one of the gang, but we captured the leader and learned that four others in teams of two were out searching for Rylee and Jessica."

"And you think the gunshots had to do with that?"

"What else? There is close to zero chance it could have been anyone else. Oliver and Gabe are trying to track them down, but we should prepare for bad news."

"Rylee's alright. She's smarter than the fools who take up what cowhands call the owl-hoot trail. And she's so tough she'd eat off the same plate as a rattler."

"You've been spending too much time with the cattlemen around here."

"They pay their bills. I know some lawyers who spend half their time working for folks who can't pay and the other half traipsing around the country looking for adventure."

He didn't take her too seriously. He carried his share of the load in the firm—well, most of the time. She was really chiding him for taking off with the posse and taking another firm lawyer with him.

The two female lawyers in the firm appeared to pay more attention to billings than he did, and he conceded that Jael had collected more fees the past year than he had. But, of course, she had Quanah Parker and the Comanche Nation as clients, and more recently several Navajo clans from the western part of the territory and eastern Arizona. The Navajo were recent visitors in no small part because she was on her way to becoming fluent in their tongue along with the other five languages she spoke. Josh spoke passable Spanish when necessary but had been known to utter an embarrassing phrase or two.

He changed the subject. "You said Michael stopped by."

"As if you didn't know before. We had a nice talk. I told him to head home and put up the mules and the bay he hopes to claim and get cleaned up and then come back into town, and I will treat the two of you to dinner at the La Castillo. I need to work late. I'll meet you there at seven o'clock. This will give you plenty of time to go home, take a bath and shave, and you can ride back into town together."

"You really do want to get the stink off me, don't you? Comanche didn't shave, and they didn't bathe much when I was around them."

"I've been spoiled by civilization, and you are not Comanche, and I am only by adoption. My parents were German Jews. We adapt to the standards of the communities in which we live." She took his hand. "And there are rewards for cleanliness."

"I will be the cleanest man you've ever slept with. Of course, if you are telling the truth, they were all Comanche." He assumed that her deceased husband, Four Eagles, had been the only one.

"All that counts is after our marriage. I have not asked for your history, and I will not give you mine."

Constanza Hildago and Jessica Chandler were the only ones who still resided in Santa Fe, and he suspected that Jael had heard gossip, or her frightening intuition had informed her. He did not want to go down this path. "Agreed."

"Now, about Michael. He told me he wants to spend the rest of the summer at Slash R. He even has visions of being a rancher. He said you had no objection."

"Well, I told him we would need to discuss this with you."

"But you don't object?"

"No, he thinks he wants to ranch. He's plenty young to decide, but a full summer might work it out of his system. If not, it sounds like he will have plenty of opportunity there."

"Do you know what he said? He told me we're never home anyway, and he does the chores around our little place in a half day. While he loves to read, he doesn't want to spend that much of his day doing it."

"Well, he has a point."

"You can't imagine what else he told me. Did he ever mention a Santa Fe girl named Sally to you?"

"No, he did not."

"He says she's a year older than he is and very pretty. She likes him a lot, and he finds her interesting, whatever that means. He thought he could go to town to see her when he finished chores, even bring her out to the ranch to ride horses. I don't like that. A girl at fifteen can be dangerous."

Josh grinned, "Yeah, I remember a few of those."

"It's not funny. I was still fifteen when I married Four Eagles. I've decided to agree to let him return to the Slash R when his Uncle Nate comes to town."

"Can I tell him that?"

"Yes, I guess so, but I don't like it."

"Well, I'll head home and take that bath and shave the whiskers. Michael and I will meet you at seven. I look forward to a nice evening back home."

He stood, and Jael slid her own chair back and got up. He took her in his arms again and kissed her. It was good to be with this challenging woman again.

Chapter 36

"WHO IS SALLY?" Josh asked.

"Sally?" Michael said.

"Yes. The Santa Fe girl you told your mother about."

"Oh, that Sally."

A bathed Michael and his still grubby father sat in the parlor. Josh leaned back in his favorite cowhide-cushioned rocker and Michael in the matching settee. "What's her last name?"

"I don't know."

"What color is her hair?"

Michael hesitated. "Uh, I guess sort of brown."

"Let's stop the games, Michael. You're not going back to the Slash R till truth gets laid out on the table. There is no Sally, is there?"

Michael unsuccessfully tried to draw his head into his shoulders like a turtle into its shell before he spoke softly. "No."

"You created Sally to convince your mom she should send you back to the ranch, didn't you?"

"Yeah."

"Well, knowing your mother, it's very unlikely you were fooling her. She's just testing you to see how far you will go with the lie."

"It wasn't really a lie. It was just a story."

"It was a lie. And I am being dishonest, too, in not telling your mother about your cousin, Katherine. Tonight, you will tell your mom the truth about the mythical Sally. I am going to casually mention your friendship with Katherine, and you are going to elaborate on that friendship, telling us about the things you do together, why you like her so much and such. I'm betting this won't change anything and that you will be returning to the Slash R when Nate shows up. But we will both walk away honest men and feel a hell of a lot better about everything." He stood up. "Now I am going to get some water boiling and get me that bath and shave this beard off. You can be thinking about our conversation."

"I lost my appetite."

"You will find it when we go to the La Castillo."

"I'll put the water on to heat and haul it up to the bath-tub when it's ready."

"I would appreciate that, son."

"I hope it's alright. I borrowed your straight edge. I used Gramps's razor at the ranch."

Josh had taken several steps up the stairway to the second floor but turned abruptly and came back down, staring at his son incredulously. "You are shaving?"

"Only every two or three days. Katherine was teasing me about my whiskers."

"We will fix you up with your own shaving supplies to take back with you. A straight edge for sure and a leather strop for sharpening." He took a deep breath and reminded himself that people could be dying out there in the mountains and that this was nothing. He and Jael would get through this together.

Chapter 37

THE PRINCE OF Santa Fe was sitting in his office staring out the window where he could see the oil streetlamps and building lanterns lighting up the town in the distance. Piece by piece he expected to own most of it someday. The news that Spiegelberg had not paid a ransom was discouraging, but the persons who could tie him to the robbery or scandal should be dead by now, hopefully the snoopy deputy U.S. marshal as well.

He was rudely yanked back from his dreams when he heard Paddy O'Meara's distinctive soft rapping. He swung the swivel chair back to the desk. "Come on in, Paddy." He hoped it was news from Hackler's bunch—good news. O'Meara wouldn't bother him this late in the evening unless he had something important to report.

When the overseer entered, the grim look on the stout man's face told him good news was not on the agenda. "What is it?"

O'Meara dropped down in the chair on the other side of the desk. "Got a report from one of my spies. He's been picking up bits and pieces in the taverns, and it ain't good."

"Well, spit it out then."

"Hackler is in the federal jail at the rear of the marshal's office. Josh Rivers with that law firm brought him in."

Hanover paled, and his stomach started churning. "I've got to think about this."

"That ain't all. Rivers had a buckboard with that deputy marshal—Paris—laid out in it. Shot up bad, they say. He was unconscious and they left him at the Rand Hospital. No word on how he's doing, but the marshal took on a special deputy to keep an eye out there and another to back up the marshal at the jail."

"What in the hell happened?"

"Best that I can piece together is that the posse caught up with Hackler's gang at the cliff dwellings, but the women went and escaped a day before the posse got there. Hackler's accused of shooting the marshal. If he dies, Hackler will likely hang unless he can make a bargain that would get him off with life in the pen. From the description they got from the bank folks, I'm guessing he kilt the young banker, too. Of course, they were hooded that day."

"And what kind of bargain would that be? I've never met the man."

"But I have more than once, and he's been to the castle to see me a couple of times. He knows who the real boss is. I don't think he'll loosen his tongue real quick. He's hoping we'll hire a lawyer for him or maybe break him out."

"Scout the jail. Figure out a way to kill the bastard. If you need to use somebody from the castle crew, pay him five hundred dollars for the job and send him on his way—or kill him when the job's done. We just can't let somebody stay around after that."

"I've got a man that's itchy for some action. Grease Kaiser's been talking about moving on anyhow, and I wouldn't want to face him in a gunfight. I'll talk to him."

"The sooner the better. But back to the women and the rest of Hackler's gang."

"It gets fuzzy there. The posse killed at least one other, and somehow the dang women must have kilt one when they made their run."

"I just don't see Jessica carrying off something like that. She's such a ladylike, delicate woman. And the young filly works in a bank. They'll die out there in the wilderness anyway."

"Well, it seems that at least four of the gang took off to track them down, and they'll likely kill the women if they're still alive when they catch up to them. Two of the posse went out to find the women, but chances are they'll be too late, and they'll be outnumbered two to one."

"I do not deal well with uncertainty. We need those women dead."

"Boss, we've just got to wait that out. We got plenty to deal with here, and we need to tend to what we can do something about. Hopefully, the two women never turn up in Santa Fe again."

They were interrupted by another rapping on the door.

"What in the hell now?" Hanover said.

O'Meara got up and opened the door a crack before stepping out. Hanover could make out only the sound of muffled voices in the hallway, and it annoyed him not to know what the interruption was about.

Shortly, O'Meara returned and set down. "I'll see what more I can learn about the posse and the deputy marshal and talk to Grease about his job. We will need a day or two to set this up. That was Dexter at the door. I think you'll have to deal with his problem on your own."

"What are you talking about?"

"He says a woman and her travel bags were dropped off at the gate by the carriage from the railroad. A little blonde woman in her mid-thirties, Dex said. Claims to be your wife. Gave her name as Earlene Hanover. She's sitting on that bench outside the gate, but ain't happy about the wait, I guess."

"Earlene? I told her to delay her arrival until I confirmed to her everything was ready. Are there children with her?"

"Dex didn't mention any."

"I don't want Earlene here right now."

"Guess you'd better tell her."

"You don't know the woman. I thought I was marrying a sweet little bird. Instead, I ended up with a rattlesnake."

"Well, I wish you luck." O'Meara wasted no time getting out of the office.

Hanover felt a headache coming on, a king-sized one. Earlene could not have chosen a worse time to appear, and now he must shore himself up for the serpent's tongue.

Chapter 38

AFTER SUMMONING ONE of the maids to help settle Earlene, he went to the castle gate, ordered the guard to open it, and walked out to the bench to greet his wife who was sitting in the darkness. He could not see her eyes but could feel their glare.

"Earlene, my dear, what a nice surprise. I'm so sorry for the misunderstanding at the gate, but if you had notified me of your plans, we would have been prepared. You didn't bring the children?" He reached out a hand to help her to her feet, but she shook it off.

"If you need to do something with your hands, take my bags. And no, I didn't bring the children. You are a stranger to them anyway."

He called to the guard, "Dalton, come take the lady's bags. Bernadine is waiting inside the door to escort the lady to her room. She will tell you where to take them."

Earlene was walking beside him to the entrance now. "I trust that you are arranging a separate room for me."

"A part of the prince's suite. A separate room for the princess connecting to the prince's room."

"Doors that lock?"

"Uh, no. That should hardly be necessary between husband and wife."

"I will sleep with my derringer within reach."

"So many women are carrying those weapons these days. It seems very unladylike to me."

"They are increasingly necessary, it seems."

One reason that he had reduced his visits to the family in Illinois the past several years was that the woman had closed her thighs like a locked vault ever since she learned about his dalliance with a saloon girl in Kansas City, who, scorned, had written to Earlene with details of what his wife considered a lewd and sick affair. She refused to believe his lies that he had never strayed before.

It had been good in the early years of their marriage. Earlene was still an enticing morsel, but even more so then, and in those days, she had been an imaginative and aggressive lover as hungry for their lovemaking as he. But then she grew suspicious of him, not only of other female relationships but of the way he earned his money, and her favors turned to wifely duty, and finally they became a weapon and were withheld. She claimed she feared the diseases he might carry.

"So, are the children coming later?"

"No."

"Why not?"

"We will talk in the morning. I am tired and will go directly to bed."

Sleep was elusive that night as Hanover lay in bed, pondering the avalanche of concerns that had swallowed him, made worse by the unexpected appearance of Earlene. He felt like he was wandering in a maze trying to find his way out, encountering dead ends at every turn. And the thought of Earlene only steps away ignited his lust.

She was a tiny thing, not more than an inch over five feet and might barely weigh one hundred pounds. He was confident he could overpower her and have his way, force her to be a real wife again. However, he knew she would use the gun without hesitation, and if he successfully removed it from her reach and made his conquest, she might go to the law. That he did not need. She obviously had a mission here, and he would listen to what she had to say. Then he would decide. He wondered if he might arrange for her disappearance.

Dawn was approaching when he finally succumbed to sleep, and when his eyes did open, the sun was sending bright shafts of light through the window. Then he remembered Earlene. He got up and tapped on the door. No answer, so he opened it enough to see the empty bed all nicely made up. For a moment, he thought her appearance might have been a nightmare, but then he heard her distinctive laugh drifting up the stairway.

He pulled on a robe and found his slippers and headed downstairs. He was upset when he got to the kitchen and saw Earlene seated at the kitchen table with Bernadine sharing coffee and pastries like old friends. It was unthinkable, his wife breakfasting with a common servant.

Bernadine started when he appeared and abandoned her chair. Hanover said, "Bernadine, you know that madam should have been served in the dining room."

"Sorry, sir." She slipped out of the room and disappeared.

Earlene said, "Don't be like that, Charles. I asked her if I could eat in the kitchen, and if she would join me. She is the first congenial soul I've encountered since I arrived, and I enjoyed her company."

"I heard you laughing from upstairs. Cackling like a hen."

"I can't even recall the last time I saw you smile, Charles. Your ill-gotten wealth apparently has not made you happy."

"You do not know where my money comes from."

"That is precisely why I have concluded it must be the result of dishonesty. Otherwise, why would it be such a secret?"

"I do not wish to discuss this right now."

"Pour yourself a cup of coffee, Charles, and sit down. We are going to have our little talk here and now. Or can you even pour a cup of coffee? I'm sure you usually have a servant take care of such things. I would get up and do that much for you."

He ignored her, picked up one of the cups laid out on the kitchen counter, took the pot off the coal stove, and poured himself a cup of coffee. He would have preferred whiskey, but he did not want to take the woman's ridicule over that.

When he sat down, he said, "I am listening."

"I came here to inform you to your face, Charles, that I am going to divorce you. I have already employed an Illinois lawyer. I will direct him to proceed with the paperwork when I return. Grounds: abandonment, adultery and whatever else he comes up with. You will have the papers served upon you by the law here, although I am told this may all take some time."

He was surprised but not especially upset by her announcement. He was tired of this woman. "The children?"

"I am assured that I will receive custody. You may come to Illinois to visit, but you will not be permitted to move them from the state."

He would employ his own lawyer to deal with this. He was determined to offer some surprises of his own. "We shall see. Our property is very complicated. That will be difficult to settle."

"No, it won't. I own the Illinois house. I have my own means of support. If I did not, we would have starved with the little you have provided us. I want nothing from you but to get out of my life. I certainly have no interest in this foolish, monstrosity of a castle you have constructed here. You have always talked about your royal heritage. That is pure bullshit. You carry no more royal blood than the big, mongrel dog the kids and I took in off the street. Only Pete is loyal and loving and would protect us with his life."

Hanover stood up, threw the remaining contents of the cup in her face, and stomped out of the room.

Chapter 39

CAL RIVERS ENTERED the marshal's office just before dusk to relieve Marshal Chance Calder. His Colt was holstered on his gun belt, but he had left his Winchester behind, thinking he would prefer the marshal's scattergun for this night's work. When he walked in, Calder was sitting at his desk, shotgun barrel resting on the desktop pointed at the doorway.

"Good evening to you, too, Chance."

Calder shifted the shotgun barrel away from Cal. "Trying to be ready. I gotta say I'm jumpy as a bit-up old bull at fly time. I hate to leave you here alone. Couldn't hire nobody else on short notice. I'll stay over in one of the cells if you want. If somebody wants to kill Hackler or break him out, I think the highest risks are tonight and tomorrow night. If Hackler is connected with this so-called Prince of Santa Fe, they'll want to do something with Hackler when they get the news about Deputy Brigham Paris."

"What news?"

"He died. Doc did the surgery and got the slug out, but it was just too late. Putrefaction had already set in and couldn't be stopped. I owe it to my fellow lawman to finish what he started. I'm thinking that he had it figured out right that this Charles Hanover is behind everything."

"I'll be danged. I didn't know. That means a likely hanging for Hackler, doesn't it?"

"Yep. A whole lot of talking might give him a chance for a life sentence, but that's up to the prosecutor and Hackler's lawyer to work out. Ain't my decision, but if it was, I'd stretch the bastard's neck."

"Does Hackler know about Paris's death yet?"

"Nope. I only got word a few hours ago. Thought I would leave that to you. I'm betting you can handle it in a way that settles more fear in his bones."

"I'm glad to do it. Make the evening a bit more interesting. You still going to have another gun outside?"

"Yeah, I got old Abe Markham set up on the roof of the drugstore across the street. He's a bit long in the tooth, but he was a buffalo hunter, and he'll have his Sharps loaded and ready."

"I'll pretend he's not there. Things can go wrong. What if they try to come through the back way?"

"That door's two inches thick and got a steel bar anchoring it. It will take some work. They won't sneak up on you, that's for dang sure."

"Okay, I'll look over your jail facilities and have a chat with Mister Hackler. They'll have to take him over my dead body."

"Don't say that. I don't like that talk. That's what I worry about."

"Just saying. I ain't planning on dying anytime soon."

"Okay. Just remember you are an acting deputy. You represent the law."

"Are you hinting I might behave less than law-like?"

"You've been known to."

"Well, don't you worry a minute, Chance. Now, why don't you just leave that scattergun on the desk and be on your way, so I can lock up."

The marshal squinted one eye and gave him a suspicious look. "You've got me worried. Why would I think you're planning something?"

"You've always been a suspicious man, Chance. I think 'Suspicious' is your middle name."

The marshal rolled his eyes and sighed. "Just don't do anything that costs me my pension." He disappeared out the front door.

Cal barred the front door and then went through the curtained entry that led to the hallway that accessed the jail cells. He was confident he had at least several hours to prepare. The prince would not send anyone to break into the jail until activity on the street had quieted or pretty much died. Of course, they would not wait for all the taverns to close, because most did not.

An oil lamp mounted on the wall just inside the entryway offered the only light in the dusky jail. He saw Hackler in one of the cells nearest the barred back door, sitting on his bunk with feet resting on the bed, back leaning against the wall and arms propped on upraised knees. His head was turned toward Cal, and Cal knew the man was appraising him with curiosity.

He walked down the hallway to the cell, pausing in front of the barred door. "Good evening, Mister Hackler, I'm your host for the night."

"Who the hell are you?"

"My name is Cal Rivers. Mister Rivers to you."

"And I'm betting you're relation to that Josh Rivers and his no-good kid, Michael."

"Brother and uncle. I have been told you had the pleasure of their company for several days."

"Humph."

"First, I wanted to inform you of the deputy U.S. marshal's condition."

"I don't give a damn what his condition is."

"You should. He's dead. The charges against you are being raised to murder. That ought to get your neck itching."

Hackler swung his legs off the bunk and got to his feet, moving nearer to Cal. "I didn't do nothing to that man. Somebody else shot him."

"That ain't my concern. Maybe you've got witnesses to contradict what the posse members will testify to."

"The man what did it is dead. They kilt him."

"You had better be thinking up a better story than that, something you can make a trade with. I'd be looking for a link to the higher-ups in your organization of outlaws."

"I don't know nothing about that."

"Too bad. Has a lawyer come around to talk to you yet?"

"You know nobody has."

"You'd think your bosses would at least send you a law wrangler. I don't suppose they figure you'll need one."

"What do you mean?"

"I'm sure they plan on killing you soon, likely tonight or tomorrow. They won't let you testify at any trial and breaking you out would be downright dumb. Then they'd have to figure out what to do with you, risk that you'd be captured again. Nope, they ain't doing that. But don't you worry. I'm here to look after you. Of course, if I got to let you go to save my own hide, I suppose I'd do it. You wouldn't be going anyplace but to the undertaker."

"You are a hell of a lawman."

"Ain't my calling. I just help out when I can. Now, you're going to have a different accommodation tonight for a spell. I want you to turn around and face the wall and put your hands behind your back."

He grabbed a pair of handcuffs hanging on a wall peg near the back door and unlocked the cell. As he stepped inside, Hackler whipped around and broke for the open cell door. Cal's fist swung down like a hammer, crushing the man's nose and dropping him to the floor on his hands and knees. Cal, a much bigger man, grasped Hackler's shirt collar, yanked him dazed and stumbling to his feet, and quickly had the wrists anchored behind his back.

Hackler's nose was bleeding profusely, and the prisoner said, "You broke my nose, and it's bleeding."

"Yep, I noticed." He pushed Hackler out of the cell and up the hallway to the office area. Then he pressed the man to the floor and cuffed his ankles.

"What are you doing? I've got to piss."

"Go right ahead. Fine with me."

"I demand a doctor. I'm going to bleed to death."

"I don't hear good."

Cal pulled his kerchief from his neck. "I hate to get your slobber and blood on my good kerchief but got no choice."

He wrapped the kerchief around Hackler's head, stuffing it in his mouth before pulling it snug and tying it. Then he opened the closet door and dragged the prisoner inside, pushed some hanging coats aside, and dropped him on the floor before closing the door.

Cal then moved the marshal's desk chair to the entrance of the jail hallway and removed the bars from the front and back doors but left the smaller bolt locks in place. He did not want access too easy from an unwelcome guest, but he preferred that the doors not be destroyed. That task completed, he retrieved the double-barreled shotgun, confirmed it was loaded and sat down in the chair, satisfying himself that he had a good view of both doors.

After little more than an hour, he dozed off with the shotgun cradled in his arms only to be awakened suddenly by a rapping on the front door. A woman's voice was screaming, "Marshal, marshal. Come quick. There's been a killing at Big Jim's Saloon."

He got to his feet and moved to the door, taking care not to get in front of it on the chance that gunfire or explosives might shatter the barrier. He hollered, "Who's out there?"

"Me, Margo from the saloon. Please, hurry."

He was not leaving the jail. If somebody was dead, there wasn't a dang thing he could do for him or her. His job was to protect the prisoner. He suspected a ruse, but he could not be certain. There was a woman named Margo who was a saloon girl at Big Jim's and led customers upstairs for better paying business when opportunity arose. He quietly released the lock and stepped away from the door, positioning himself so he would be behind it when it opened. "Come on in and tell me about it."

The door opened, and the first thing he saw was a hand clutching a Colt pistol. He threw his shoulder into the door, slamming it back onto the intruder. The Colt clattered to the floor, and the man's grunt told him he had made a solid strike. He pulled the door open again, and a solidly built man fell forward into the office, landing face-down on the floor. He stepped out just in time to see a skirted figure rushing down the street, obviously a woman who had been paid or coerced to visit the marshal's office. He would give Chance Calder Margo's name, and he could follow up as he saw fit.

He stepped onto the boardwalk, studying the roof of the building across the street. No sign of Abe Markham who could have at least fired a warning shot in the direction of the visitor. Sleeping, unconscious or dead, he supposed. He dragged the would-be killer out of the open doorway and closed and locked the door. He rolled the man over, and he moaned. Middle-aged, short man with a balding pate and thick mustache and a good week's crop of whiskers covering chin and cheeks. His hat must have flown off when the door struck. His forehead displayed a growing welt encasing a gash from the door's impact.

The man was moaning now, and he needed to get him into a cell. The thought was abruptly interrupted by an explosion at the jail's rear. He rushed to the hallway entrance and saw a tall man with a black, wide-brimmed hat and handlebar mustache step through the smoke nearly hiding the shattered door, a dandy with a six-gun in each hand. He readied the shotgun. "Keep it low," he whispered to himself, and squeezed the trigger the instant the invader saw him.

The shotgun's roar was followed by the gunman's screams. Cal turned to see the other man crawling toward the gun he had lost when the door walloped him. He hurried to the gunman's side and drove the shotgun butt onto the top of his hand, flattening it on the floor. The crunch of shattered bone was followed by an agonizing scream, so that Cal now had a chorus of screaming in the jailhouse. He found another set of handcuffs in the marshal's desk and locked them on the man's wrists, picked up the pistol, tucked it in his belt, and moved to the outlaw in the cell room, his shotgun at the ready in case the man needed another dose of buckshot to shut him up.

The smoke was clearing now, and he saw no sign of others outside. It seemed unlikely there would be more than the two, but he would still be cautious. He suspected with noise from the office, word would get to the marshal quickly and that Chance would arrive soon.

He approached the gunslinger slowly. "Toss your guns down the hallway, mister, if you don't want a second dose."

"Don't know where the damn things are at. Dropped them when the buckshot hit. Don't care none. I'm a dead man. Think you shot my balls off. You're a sick son-of-a-bitch." The gunman started sobbing.

Cal saw the guns as he drew nearer, both well out of the man's reach. He was leaning back against the bars of a cell, his shredded legs splayed out on the floor almost swallowed by a pool of blood. He picked up the guns.

"I need a doc," the gunslinger said, "now."

"What's your name?"

"Kaiser. Orville Kaiser. Some call me 'Grease.'"

"Because of your speed with the draw, I suppose."

"Yeah. And you didn't give me a chance."

"I don't play those kid's games. I'm more into staying alive."

Kaiser moaned, "I don't want to die. I need a doc."

Cal said, "Yeah, we'll get you one in due course." He heard a frantic pounding on the door from the front and turned away and headed back up the hallway.

"Cal, open up. Are you alright in there? Answer me." It was Marshal Chance Calder yelling.

He unlocked the door, and the marshal rushed in.

"Damn, Cal. You had me sick with worry."

"You could've come in the back. The door was open."

"What do you mean?"

"The man back there must work with explosives some. I'm guessing a small stick of dynamite. Anyhow, you'll have a door to replace."

"You said you've got a man in back. Who's this man?" He nodded toward the dazed outlaw on the floor.

"Ain't been introduced formally yet. He tried to hit me from the front. Had to bash his head with the door. Then he tried to go for the gun he'd dropped, and I had to slap his hand. Now, he'll live despite the fuss he's making. Feller in back I ain't so sure about. Tried to keep him alive so you could talk to him. I suppose we ought to get Doc Rand over here. It's after midnight. He probably won't like it much. I'll go over to his place and roust him if you like."

The marshal brushed past Cal and marched over to the hallway and looked at the cell room. "My prisoner. Where is he? Please don't tell me he escaped."

"Oh, I about forgot about him. He's hiding in the closet." Cal stepped over and opened the closet door. "I'll just leave these folks to you while I mosey over to Doc's and get him moving."

He started out the door, and then turned back to the marshal. "Oh, what about Abe Markham? I ain't heard a peep from him."

Calder looked like he wanted to crawl under the desk. "I checked on him. He's up on the roof. Dead. Dead drunk I should say. Sorry."

"You gave me real good backup, Chance. The least you could do is give me the old fart's pay."

"Done."

Chapter 40

I T HAD TAKEN almost another week to reach the Rio Chama. Rylee knew she and Jessica had likely cost the hikers at least two days, but she was confident that both were doing better. Jessica was toughening up some, gaining strength and adapting to the primitive life that had been forced upon her. Occasionally, she slipped into silence and was obviously depressed. Rylee assumed that her new friend still suffered from the loss of her baby.

Rylee could not see the wound in the back of her thigh, but Wolf checked it daily and assured her there was no putrefaction and that it was healing nicely. She used a walking stick to ease the weight on the leg a bit, and the first few days, the pain when she walked had been on the edge of unbearable, but it had faded now to mere annoyance.

Now that they had the comforts of a fire when they stopped at the end of a day's travel, they did not freeze at night. Of course, she and Gabe snuggled together chastely under shared blankets. Wolf had surrendered two blankets to Jessica but seemed to have no problem curling up near the fire, which he tended through the night, and snatching the sleep he needed. Such a strange, quiet man.

Best of all, they no longer starved. Wolf and Gabe kept them supplied with venison and rabbit, even a turkey once, and she harvested plants to supplement their meals. Gabe had surprised her with his comfort in the wilderness and display of hunting and survival skills. During this journey, she was learning more daily about the man she loved, and she liked what he was revealing. Perhaps a couple never stopped discovering things about each other. That would make life more interesting.

This adventure reminded her that life was fragile and that moments with those we love should be treasured, as Gabe had already suggested. Perhaps he was right, and it was time to capture more of those moments.

Wolf and Gabe had disappeared into the timber seeking downed trees that might be fashioned into a raft. There were ample trees about them, but they had no axe or saw. Rylee and Jessica were harvesting vines that might be used to bind the logs into a floatable craft. They had already found a clearing on a rise above the Chama, and Rylee had started a fire at the campsite where they would spend the night. There was a variety of good firewood here, especially oak and hackberry among the ponderosa pine and juniper that did not burn so well.

The river below was beautiful as it flowed through the valley and did not appear too threatening, but Wolf had promised to tell them more about the river later. He had followed most of the river's course, sketching and painting as he traveled. Much of his work these days consisted of commissions for specific subjects, but paintings and sketches available to the public were displayed at the Teatro Santa Fe, and she hoped she could identify one of the Rio Chama there. She would love to invest in one for their home. "Their" home? Yes, the one she would share with Gabe.

By late afternoon, Wolf and Gabe had found and half-carried and half-rolled three logs to the river's side and now were binding them to form a raft. Their lengths varied by a foot or two, the shortest being about ten feet but the diameters of each were roughly a foot and a half. They were sturdy mountain mahogany not yet damaged by rot. The raft would be a slender craft that would be easier to negotiate stones and narrows through Chama Canyon the next day, Wolf said.

The raft was ready for service before sundown, and now they were seated on the ground around the fire, roasting venison on sticks, Rylee and Gabe sharing one side. As they ate, they talked about the remainder of their journey back to Santa Fe.

Rylee asked Wolf, "How long do you expect it to take for us to get home?"

"With luck, we will only have one night on the river. That assumes we can go most of the day tomorrow and we don't run into something unexpected. By noon the next day we should reach the convergence of Rio Chama with the Rio Grande. We should be in Santa Fe by nightfall. There are cabins and small ranches along the riverside once we near the merging of the rivers. We can consider if we want to try to rent some horses if the raft isn't holding up, but otherwise I would wait till we get nearer to Santa Fe. Folks will be less concerned about getting their critters back closer to home."

"You mentioned something 'unexpected.' For example?"

"Getting tossed off the raft in rapids for instance. The raft would go on without us if that happens. Or if one or two of us go off, the others would be forced to land the raft and wait or hike back and help. Or we might run into a bunch of bears fishing and be forced to pull in and wait till they're done."

Gabe said, "In Louisiana where I come from, it's alligators."

Rylee said, "How much of a threat are the rapids?"

Wolf said, "These aren't as mean as a lot of rivers and not so many, but they can be like breaking a wild horse sometimes. The river's not over your head most places, even shallow in others. You might have noticed that Gabe and I found some downed tree limbs and cut off the branches as best we could with our knives. We'll each have one to help us control the raft or push us off a sandbar or out of mud. Don't worry, we'll get there, but it could take an extra day or two if things go bad."

Later, Rylee lay on her side with Gabe spooned up against her backside. Sleep evaded her. Too many things to think about. Poor Willi Spiegelberg. He must be worried sick. She was keenly aware that she was the child he never had, and with her parents' deaths, he was something of a father figure to her. Josh and Jael would be anxious, too. There were bank customers that needed her attention. And what was happening to the so-called Prince of Santa Fe? She sighed. And what about her and Gabe?

"Rylee, are you alright?" Gabe whispered in her ear.

"Yes. I'm okay. I'm just thinking maybe it's time."

"Now. Right here where Oliver and Jessica can see and hear us?" He snuggled closer and wrapped his arm tighter around her, his fingers moving to her breast.

She could tell he was horny and probably would not be deterred by the risk of an audience. Well, she was, too, but she was not going to perform for an audience. She gave him a sharp elbow to the ribs. "Put your brains back in your head. I am talking about marriage."

He moved his hand away but not too far. "What about marriage?"

"You have asked me to marry you so often I've lost count. When I said it's time, I was talking about us getting married unless you've changed your mind."

"Oh, yeah. You want to get married?"

"Ask me again and find out?"

He whispered in her ear. "I love you, Rylee O'Brian. Will you marry me?"

She rolled over and kissed him. "And I love you, Gabriel Laurent. Yes, I will marry you."

"When do you have in mind? Six months? A year?"

"One week after we get back to Santa Fe. Wedding at the Rivers house. No more than a dozen or so guests. I will move into your house until we find something with more space. We both have money saved back. We shouldn't need a loan. I must catch up at the bank, and you will owe the law firm time, so there will be no honeymoon trip. Hold off on babies for two years, but if there's an accident, I think we will be able to afford a nanny, so I'm not forced to give up my bank position."

"Well, you sent my brains back to my head. As usual, you've got everything planned out it seems."

"That's a problem?"

"Nope. I knew what I was getting into. Can you sleep now?"

"Yes, I'm sure I can."

Chapter 41

THE RIO CHAMA flowed gently for the first few hours of their journey. The raft's occupants had no control over the speed of the crude vessel, and it was a leisurely cruise that Gabe did not mind. He was certain that Rylee, who sat in front of him, would be impatient, however. Wolf had suggested that Gabe take the aft position because of his experience rafting over the years and the rear of a raft tended to be most critical to guiding the watercraft. Wolf was in the fore spot with Jessica behind him.

It did not surprise him when Rylee said, "It will take us years to get to Santa Fe at this pace."

"Just enjoy the view. We must be entering the Chama Canyon that Oliver mentioned. That canyon wall just ahead must rise to well over a thousand feet above the river. This can be our honeymoon trip."

"Not funny."

Suddenly the river narrowed to less than half the nearly thirty feet width they had been floating on, and the speed of the water flow doubled. "Hang on," he hollered. "Trouble ahead."

Huge boulders were scattered at random on the riverbed and the water deepened. Ahead, he saw that the canyon walls jutted out and extended into the river forming a narrow alley for the water to rush through, and one could only guess what obstacles lay beneath the surface. The raft plowed into the narrows and the swirling waves of white water and shot through the opening. Gabe doubted that a wider vessel could have made it through the chute-like gap.

He saw daylight ahead where the canyon walls receded and moved back from the river's edge. They catapulted out of the gap, the front of the raft driving into a boulder and flipping the crude vessel on its side, tossing the occupants aside like rag dolls. Gabe landed in deep water, but stroked with the current to the bank, looking around for the others as he swam.

He saw Oliver grasping Jessica's hand and lifting her from the river which was widening now and shallow along the channel's edges. The raft was wedged into some rocks on the opposite side which would have been no more than twenty feet distant at this point. His heart raced. Rylee. Where was Rylee?

He said, "Oliver, did you see Rylee?"

"No. Maybe she's behind the raft. I'll go over and check."

Then Gabe saw her in the water downstream, bouncing over the rocks with the white water. She swam like a fish ordinarily, but her body was lifeless, and she was making no effort to escape the current. "She's going down river. I've got to catch her." He pulled off his soaked boots and peeled off his shirt and britches and dived into the icy water. He allowed the fast-flowing current to carry him, stroking only to dodge the stones and occasional tree and brush jams that got in his way.

The river snaked through the canyon, and Rylee disappeared around a bend. When he negotiated the water's twist, he could no longer see her. Had she disappeared beneath the surface, sucked in by a whirlpool, perhaps, like one that tried to capture him? He was on the verge of panic. He loved that woman more than life. He was about to continue his quest downstream when he spotted her on a shelf of sandstone that extended into the water's edge. Motionless, but he had found her. He swam toward the bank until his feet could feel the shale and gravel of the river bottom. Then he stood and splashed through the water to get to her side.

Instantly, he saw the nasty, bleeding gash on the side of her head. When he knelt beside her, he feared at first she was dead, but then he saw the labored rise and fall of her chest and heard the choking sound from her throat. He pulled her up on the sandbar and placed her face down on the sand and shale. He started pressing on her back between the shoulder blades, and she coughed. Water ran from her mouth, and he continued, grateful to receive a moan and more coughing.

Finally, he helped her sit up. Her eyes fixed on him questioningly. "Just cough," he said. "Take deep breaths."

"I've...got to puke." She started vomiting, making no effort to miss her soaked clothes.

He figured he could rinse the garments off in the river. It was late morning, and the bright sun was igniting a giant fireplace in the canyon. He had learned that the mountain air dried clothes twice as fast as the humid Louisiana climate.

Rylee was sitting up on her own accord now, still choking and coughing, her flawless, tawny skin as pale as he had ever seen it, but he no longer feared for her life. "We've got to get you out of those wet clothes. It appears you lost your moccasins in the river."

She looked up at him. "You're always trying to get me out of my clothes."

Her remark told him she was doing fine. "I want to lay them over some boulders or tree limbs to dry. My undershorts go there, too."

"I guess that makes sense. What did you do with the rest of your clothes?"

"I took them off before I went into the water after you. I'm hoping Oliver and Jessica will be along and bring me something to wear, too."

"They are alright then?"

"They'll have to get the raft out of the rocks. I don't know how much repair is needed, but I'm sure they'll be along sooner or later. Now, off with the clothes and then I'll look at that knot on your head. It's not bleeding so much now. I'd rather not wrap it until we get something dry to use. If the blood isn't a problem, it might be just as well not to put a compress on it."

They were sitting side by side on the sandbar, Rylee resting her head against Gabe's shoulder, when they saw the raft floating around the bend. Wolf and Jessica, who sat at the rear of the raft, each had poles, so Wolf must have saved the two that Gabe did not see floating down the river. They would search out two more before they left this place.

"Good Lord, what will they think, the two of us sitting here naked as newborns?" Rylee said.

"They'll think we're drying our clothes. I have a hunch they'll be doing the same. I just hope they brought mine."

Wolf and Jessica poled the raft to sandbar's edge, and Wolfe signaled for Gabe to help. They pulled the front up onto to the bar, so the water would not catch it and carry away their transportation.

Wolf said, "We were praying that Rylee would be okay. It didn't look good when she took off downriver."

"She came near to drowning. She must have hit her head on a rock and was unconscious most of her trip. Thankfully, the river decided to spit her out onto that sandstone shelf, or I'm afraid she would have been all the way to the Rio Grande before I caught up with her."

"She would not have been alive."

"But she is. She's got a cut and knot on the side of her head. You can look at it, but I'm inclined to leave it alone since we can't stitch it. Doc can examine it and see what he thinks, but it will probably be too late for his work. She'll likely have another little scar as a souvenir."

"Well, your wet clothes are on the raft if you want to get them started drying." He looked at Jessica. "I guess we'd better strip down and get our things drying, too."

Jessica shrugged. "Getting naked in front of this bunch is nothing compared to what I've been through the past ten days. I just want to get dry."

"My matches won't do anything now," Wolf said, "but there is plenty of flint hereabouts. I'll get a fire started before nightfall. The river ate our rifles. Sidearms are drenched and so is the ammunition. The guns will need a good cleaning before they're fired again. I don't think I can bring down a deer with a pistol anyhow."

"I just want to sleep," Rylee said, curling up on her shale and sand bed.

She wasn't coughing much now, and Gabe figured rest was the best medicine for her. "Go right ahead. You're entitled, and I assume we won't be moving on today."

Wolf said, "No. We need to dig up some vines and do some repairs to the raft. I was worried it would split apart before we found you. Losing a day is a small thing compared to how this all might have turned out. We'll have a few rapids to ride yet but nothing quite like that place where the canyon walls try to come together."

"Yeah. Now I'm going to hang up my clothes, so I can get decent again."

Chapter 42

JOSH WAS AWAKENED by a hammering on the front door. He sat up in bed, trying to clear his head. He got up, stumbling around the room searching for his undershorts and trousers. A shirt would be nice, but he did not know where Jael tossed it when she was disrobing him. The savage in her came out when she was hungry for her man. For the most part, he liked that, but she had worn him out last night. Now she was cocooned naked in the blankets and oblivious to the world. He had settled for his share of a sheet and part of a blanket since Jael tended to be a blanket hog.

He heard muffled voices now in the parlor and stumbled to the chest of drawers and found clean underwear and socks, stepping on his trousers dropped in a heap on the floor. He was fastening his belt buckle when he heard the light tapping on the bedroom door. "Dad, Marshal

Calder is waiting in the parlor. Says it's urgent that he talks with you." It was Michael.

"Tell him I will be five minutes."

"I told him that from all the noise you were making last night, you and mom must have been up mighty late."

Now, he would have to listen to Calder's banter. Jael's head popped from her blanket nest. "Did he say what I thought he said?" she whispered.

"I don't know what you thought he said, but he told the marshal we were a bit rowdy last night. You do get noisy sometimes."

She tossed a pillow at him. "I'll never get back to sleep now. I'd just as well get up."

"Well, don't walk out into the parlor naked."

Josh grabbed a fresh shirt from the closet, pulling it on as he went out the bedroom door.

Michael was still in the hallway. "I was just joshing," he said. "I didn't really tell the marshal you were up late." He gave that impish grin that had a way of dissolving anger. "You did make kind of a racket, though, especially Mom."

"Discuss it with your mother. She's the one that's going to be after your hide."

Josh stepped into the parlor and found Marshall Chance Calder sitting in Josh's favorite rocker, hat tugged down on his forehead like he might be sleeping. Josh sat down on the stuffed couch on the opposite side of the sturdy oak coffee table that separated the furniture pieces. "Good morning, Chance."

"Morning, Josh. I thought slavery ended with the war."

"What do you mean?"

"Michael saw me on the veranda hammering on the door, and he came up from the stable. Said he was tending to the critters. Expecting a lot of a boy to get out before the sun's up to work like that."

"If Michael was out working already, that was his choice. Jael and I see to chores when Michael's not here, and during the school year, we all pitch in. And why in the hell am I explaining this to you anyhow? What are you doing here at this ungodly hour?"

"Michael put a pot of coffee on the stove when I got here. It should be ready."

Josh was struggling with his sense of humor this morning, but he got up and returned with two mugs after delivering one to the bedroom for Jael. She was nearly dressed but indicated she did not plan to join his conversation with the marshal. She intended to slip out the back door and help Michael at the stable.

Josh placed the steaming cups on the table. "Now, what's your story?"

"Had you heard that Deputy Paris died?"

"Yes. Danna stopped by Doc's office, and he asked her to tell me. I got word just before I left the office. I'm sorry about that. It took a spell, but I came to like and respect the man. He was set on doing his duty."

"Yeah. I sent a telegram to the Marshals Service. I assume we'll bury him in Santa Fe. A graveside gathering, I suppose. I'm hoping to hear from the service about any special religious rites, and they'll notify family. He never talked about anyone."

"Somehow, I don't feel this is what you are here to talk about."

"Time for us to visit the prince. I'd like you to go with me this afternoon. I'd welcome a law wrangler's tongue, although some say they're all forked."

Josh ignored the jab. "I don't have anything scheduled at the office till tomorrow. Nobody knew when—or if—I would be back. Something triggered your decision to do this just now."

"Got me another witness, and this one's loosening his tongue fast. I can thank your brother Cal. He took watch at the jail last night and set himself a trap."

"That sounds like Cal."

"Took down two men that showed up to kill Hackler. One—he goes by Grease Kaiser—bunked at the castle and knows plenty. Cal gave him a load of buckshot below the waist so his mouth would keep working. Doc's caring for him at the jail. The other feller is a saddle tramp that got hired on by Grease to cause a diversion—I think that's what you call it. He don't know nothing."

"So what are we going to do with the prince?"

"We're going to make an arrest. Hackler and Kaiser can build a solid chain for the prosecutors, and I'm thinking there will be a fight over which jurisdiction gets first chance at him. I don't give a dang. I just want him out of Santa Fe dead or alive."

"He's got gunfighters there. Are we taking on the whole bunch?"

"Cal will be outside with four or five men. If he hears a gunshot, they'll be crashing through the gate."

"That doesn't help much if the first gunshot takes down one of us."

"Fort Marcy don't have many troops these days, but the commanding officer said he could get me thirty or so cavalrymen to line up on horseback some distance back from the castle's entrance. This is a civilian matter, so they won't enter any fight. This will be a drill for them. But their presence will send a message. And if fired upon, they will respond."

"Now that's pretty good thinking, Chance. I don't think they'll be wanting to take on the Army. Sounds like fun. Where do we meet?"

"Come by the office shortly after one o'clock. Cal and the others will be there, and I'll explain in more detail what I've got in mind."

Josh started when Jael spoke from behind him. "It doesn't sound too bad. I just want to see this finished up. Michael and I will be riding with Cal's men. A few more numbers won't hurt. Chance, why don't you stay for breakfast? I've got some pastries I bought from the new bakery, and I can fry some eggs and bacon. It won't take but a bit. Josh, why don't you call Michael up from the stable for breakfast? I have a few morning appointments, so I'll have to ride to the office and change there. You can spend some time with Michael this morning and bring him in and take me out for lunch."

As Josh walked to the stable to fetch Michael, he just shook his head in disbelief. He simply could not keep up with that wife of his. She was like a dang cat, one minute all over you demanding love and affection, the next moving on to stalking prey or racing through the house chasing an imagined foe. Don't even try to guess the cat's plans at a given moment or think you have her routine figured out. You will be wrong. Just love her for what she is.

Chapter 43

I T WAS NOT quite sunrise when a naked Charles Hanover crept over to the door that separated Earlene's room from his. He wanted her, and she was his wife, so he decided she would perform her wifely duty to satisfy his early morning lust. He turned the doorknob and pushed, but it did not budge. She had pushed the chair up against the door. It was next to worthless to deter someone who was determined to enter, and he was nothing if not determined.

He drove his shoulder into the door, wincing at the pain but elated when the chair slid away and the door opened, and he stepped into the shadowy room. He could make out Earlene on the bed, not sitting up yet, obviously disoriented. He charged the bed and pounced on her, pinning her down with one hand while he tugged the blankets away with the other.

He grunted when he felt her long, sharp fingernails rake down one cheek and again when her claws dug into his shoulder.

"Get off of me, you bastard," she said. "Get your filthy body away from me." Her knee came up and struck a glancing blow to his genitals. It hurt but was not the sickening, disabling strike it might have been, but the thought of what she attempted enraged him and his hands went to her throat. His fingers tightened and he began to squeeze. Her arms thrashed and flailed, trying to fight him off but soon weakened and collapsed and her body went limp.

He eased his grip now. He was not certain if she was dead or alive, but he pulled her gown off, spread her thighs and quickly found release. When he got off her, she was starting to stir. Should he finish his work and kill her? His hands moved toward her throat again when he suddenly thought better of it. How would he dispose of a body without the intervention of the law? How might others in the castle use Earlene's death to blackmail him? No, it was all too complicated.

He rolled away and got up and returned to his room, closing the door to shut off the sound of her moaning. He was more relaxed now, starting to think more clearly. He was hungry, but the cook would not have breakfast ready for at least an hour. Paddy O'Meara was to join him then with a report on Hackler's fate. He had already enjoyed a fine start to his day, and he expected the news to enhance it even more.

He found a handkerchief and wiped it over his burning shoulder, drawing back a bloody cloth. It was like a damn bear had attacked hm. He had a pitcher of water and a bowl on the vanity and took another handkerchief and washed the wound as well as the scratches on his face. The sunlight was sifting through the curtains now, lighting the room, and he studied the scratch marks in the mirror. They were beginning to scab over already but would be an ugly sight for a week or so. This morning, he would need to shave carefully around them.

He shaved and cleaned up, allowing time for the shoulder wound to dry, hoping the blood would not soak through his shirt. As was his practice, he dressed in suit and tie. Before going downstairs to breakfast, he opened Earlene's door and peered in. She sat on the bed, leaning against the headboard, her blankets pulled tight about her. She said nothing, just glared at him, her lips formed in a pout.

"You could have made it easy, you know," he said. "I want you out of the house today. You will need to find a hotel room to stay in until you make train connections.

You will be hearing from my lawyer. I will fight for custody of my son, of course." The thought occurred to him that things would have been simpler had he killed her. Better though if she died at the hotel. Yes, that could be arranged. Perhaps she could pleasure him again, and he would kill her himself. There had been something erotic about this morning's encounter.

Silence.

He shrugged and closed the door.

O'Meara was already at the breakfast table when Hanover entered the dining room and took his place at the head of the table. O'Meara, grim-faced, nodded and continued eating his hotcakes and sausage. O'Meara rarely smiled, so Hanover did not consider the sour face a particular concern. Still, there was something about the man's demeanor that made him uneasy.

The cook, a buxom, younger olive-skinned woman brought a steaming cup of coffee and plate of hotcakes and sausages for Hanover and placed them on the table. "Anything else, senor?" she said.

"No, thank you, Margarita. Mister O'Meara and I require some privacy. Do you understand?"

She nodded. "Si senor." She scurried out of the room.

O'Meara said, "You do know she speaks English better than we do, me anyhow."

"I've had her in the kitchen six months now. She always seems to have trouble understanding me."

"Probably figures you expect it. Her pa is out of New York and been a trader here for years. Her ma's Mexican."

"I'll never understand these people. Tell me about Hackler. We got rid of him, I trust."

"We did not. Didn't touch him. Grease got himself shot and is in jail now, too. You can thank Cal Rivers again. I don't know much, but he set some kind of trap figuring we'd try to get to Hackler."

"We just made things worse."

"I wouldn't disagree with that. Grease has been living here at the castle. He knows a hell of a lot more than Hackler. I'm moving on first thing tomorrow morning. You still owe me nearly three thousand dollars. I'm guessing you got gold coin stashed in that office safe, and I'm wanting my money before the day's out."

"You son-of-a-bitch. You're a damned traitor, a deserter. I don't owe you a nickel."

"You owe me, and I'll be in to collect. Let's say three o'clock."

Hanover pushed his breakfast plate aside. His stomach would rebel if he tried to eat, and his appetite had disappeared. He felt cold and weak and did not know if it was more rage or fear that had taken over and was devouring him. "Get out of my sight."

O'Meara drank the last of his coffee and got up. "Three o'clock."

Hanover went directly to his office. He had to think this out. He sat down at his desk and stared out the window overlooking the grounds in front of the castle. He could see the guard at the gate and another walking along the parapet. He had close to a dozen men here to defend the castle, and he doubted the marshal could come up with that many. Perhaps he could yet escape, but he needed help. The safe contained nearly twenty thousand dollars. He hated O'Meara now, but when they talked later, he would make a deal with the man. They would divide the money if O'Meara would guide him to Mexico. O'Meara knew folks, had traveled the Southwest.

But how did he know the man would not turn on him and take everything? He would ponder this, give him an incentive. He thought of himself as a supremely clever man. He would come up with a new enterprise and sell O'Meara on it. They would partner fifty-fifty, maybe engage in a legitimate business if they could find something that would yield good money. He might even find a woman there to help with language barriers and share his bed.

What about his children? He could live without them just fine. He would need to abandon the royalty game, as he doubted that the Mexicans would give a damn about a British prince. Americans had not seemed impressed either, and he was ready to concede a lost cause. But he must leave this place soon, today if possible. He would find Paddy and talk to him yet this morning. They would just disappear without a word to anyone. With luck, the law would not be seeking him out for days, and he would vanish before that U.S. marshal gave him a thought.

He searched the castle but did not find O'Meara till he appeared at the dining table for lunch. He figured the fool would show up for mealtime. The hired guns all ate at a separate cookhouse on the grounds where Rosa, Margarita's mother, presided with her thirteen-year-old grandson as an assistant. A prince did not dine with lowly soldiers.

There was a prolonged silence as the men dined on steak, fried potatoes and fresh-baked bread. Hanover hated Mexican food, although it was included on the menu for his hires because cost was less, and they seemed to like it well enough. Finally, Hanover spoke. "I accept your pulling out of here, but I have got a proposition."

O'Meara looked up from his plate and squinted at him. "I'm listening."

"Take me with you."

"Take you with me? Are you crazy?"

"Lead me into Mexico to a safe place there. Stay on, and we will start up a new business south of the border. I'll split the money in my safe, well over ten thousand dollars each. I have money in a half dozen banks. We ought to be able to figure out how to get some of that. I'll give you a ten percent commission for helping recover the other funds."

He could tell that O'Meara was pondering this development. The conversation ended when Earlene entered and sat down at the far end of the table opposite him, her steel-gray eyes boring in with hatred. The side of her face was red and swollen. The top button on her blouse was unfastened and the neck rolled down a bit, evidently to exhibit the red and purplish marks on the flesh about her throat. Bitch. She was advertising the results of this morning's encounter. He should have finished the job since he would be disappearing anyway. He still might if he caught her alone someplace.

Margarita entered the dining room with a plate for Earlene and froze for a moment when she saw his wife's face. She set the plate in front of Earlene. "I'll bring fresh coffee soon." She turned and looked at Hanover, her eyes judgmental, her lips pressed tightly, before she wheeled and walked out of the room.

He saw that O'Meara was studying Earlene's face. He said nothing and returned to his meal. "We will take this up in my office after we eat."

O'Meara nodded.

Margarita returned with three slices of cake on a tray and set the plates in front of the diners. She served Earlene last. "Ma'am. I have some salve that would relieve your pain some if you wish to come into the kitchen after you have finished eating."

"Thank you, Margarita. I will do that."

After Margarita returned to the kitchen, Hanover said, "Earlene, you do remember that you are to vacate your room and this castle today?"

She looked at him as if he were beyond contempt and did not reply.

After eating the two men went to Hanover's office. When they got there and started to sit down, Hanover tossed a glance out the window and froze. "Paddy, what's going on out there?"

O'Meara joined him at the window. "Cavalry, a near company, it appears, lined up for battle. Two men riding toward the gate. One's the U.S. marshal. I've seen him around town. Don't recognize the other feller. Then in front of the soldiers, there's seven or eight other riders. They must be law."

"The guards are calling the men to the ramparts."

"You ain't going to whip those forces, I'm telling you. And you sure as hell don't want to declare war on the United States Army."

"Get down there and find out what the devil is going on. Don't let the men just surrender."

"I think the men will do what they dang well please right now. A lot of them have paper out on them but not many the hanging type. I doubt they're going to commit suicide."

"Go down and see what is going on. Report back."

"I'm going because I want to know. Your days of giving orders are done, Mister Prince. Best you can hope for is to be the court jester."

After O'Meara left the office, Hanover retrieved his gun belt from the wall peg and buckled it about his waist, slipping his Colt revolver from its holster to confirm the chambers were all loaded. Then he pulled out his bottom desk drawer and plucked out the smaller Smith & Wesson with the three-inch barrel and slipped it into his inner coat pocket. He could handle weapons and had killed a good number of men and a few women. He could not endure a trial and the waiting for a hanging, and they could not hang him more than once. If he could not escape, others would die this day. He stepped out into the hallway and walked down the stairway to the great hall and stood in the entryway, prepared to greet his guests.

Chapter 44

JOSH RODE TO Marshal Calder's left as they approached the castle's gated entrance. There were men with rifles a dozen or so feet above the ground spread out along the parapet, but none appeared ready to fire, and he did not see them as threatening at this point. Calder's ploy with the soldiers was obviously having its intended effect.

When they reached the heavy metal gate that looked like jail bars with pointed tops, a man swung it open, and another stepped out from behind the wall and moved into the opening. He was a beefy man and seasoned military, Josh judged from his bearing.

"I'm Paddy O'Meara, former top sergeant in the U.S. Army. Will you identify yourselves and state your business?"

O'Meara no doubt expected to gain some credibility by stating his former military status, and he was correct, although the marshal had served as well albeit Confederate. O'Meara had no trace of Southern accent, and his speech carried more Irish lilt. The Irish males for some reason had gravitated to the Army upon their entry into the country.

Calder responded. "I am United States Marshal Chance Calder, and this is acting Deputy Marshal Joshua Rivers. Our business is with Charles Hanover."

"That does not inform me of the nature of the business so I can advise Mister Hanover."

"If you must know, we are here to arrest him. He will face charges in New Mexico for murder and kidnapping and others too numerous to recite. The kidnapping charges may be upgraded to murder depending on facts yet to be determined. I also have orders from the Marshals Service to hold him to face charges in several states. I want you to escort us to Mister Hanover and I will make the formal arrest."

The former Army sergeant seemed unexpectedly calm about the matter, Josh thought.

Calder continued. "I gather you carry some authority here."

"You might say I am Hanover's second in command, but I deny participation in any crimes."

Josh figured O'Meara was informing them that he had knowledge that could make him an important witness. He left those issues to the marshal, however.

Calder said, "We'll have a serious conversation about your involvement later. Given your position, you should now direct your hired guns to throw down their weapons, climb down from the wall and march out front and line up. I will signal my deputies to ride up and take them into custody."

"Yes, sir. I can do that." He gave instructions to the gate guards to carry out the orders. The guards were noticeably relieved. They had not likely relished the thought of taking on the company of soldiers.

Calder signaled Cal to bring his riders to the castle, and they reined their mounts forward. The marshal spoke to O'Meara. "Now, it's time for you to introduce me to the Prince of Santa Fe."

"He's likely in his office if he's not hiding out someplace. Follow me."

They followed O'Meara and climbed stone steps onto the massive, columned portico, where he opened one of the huge double doors and waved them inside. O'Meara's eyes widened in surprise when they were met by an impeccably dressed man with carefully trimmed mustache and goatee and a vacant stare coming from pale blue eyes.

Josh had no doubt that this man was the prince, Charles Hanover. The gun belt buckled over his coat seemed out of place, and he suspected this was not ordinary attire.

"Welcome to Hanover Castle," the man said. "I am Prince Charles Hanover. To what do I owe the honor of your visit?"

Marshal Calder said, "I am United States Marshal Chance Calder, and I am here to place you under arrest for a long list of crimes including murder, bank robbery, and kidnapping, among others."

"Oh, my goodness. You must reconsider. I hate to see you make a fool of yourself."

"Now just unbuckle your gun belt and let it drop to the floor." The marshal started unclipping a pair of handcuffs attached to his own belt.

"Why certainly," Hanover said. "I always try to accommodate the law." His fingers moved toward the belt buckle, and then suddenly, fast as a lightning strike, his Colt was out of its holster, and he got off two shots.

Josh had his own weapon drawn and ready to fire when Hanover's pistol clattered on the floor, and he lifted his hands. He turned to Calder expecting to find him crumpled dead on the floor, but the marshal was still standing, handcuffs in one hand and six-gun in the other. The body on the floor was Paddy O'Meara's. Josh stepped over and knelt beside the still form knowing there was nothing to be done for the man. O'Meara had tumbled backwards upon the slugs' impact and was stretched out on his back. One slug had torn into his right eye, the other his throat. Death would have been instantaneous.

"He was a traitor," Hanover said, speaking softly.

Josh looked up from his position next to O'Meara's body. He saw Hanover's hand disappear under his coat. "Chance," he yelled, "he's got another gun."

Josh had always been slower than a turtle on the pistol draw, and before his Colt left his holster, a shot echoed in the great hall, and then another and another. Hanover had vaulted forward, dropping the pistol in his hand and lay splayed on the floor, three blood spots widening on the back of his coat.

He could not believe what he saw. A tiny blonde woman holding a pistol at her side staring at the prince's corpse.

Calder said, "Ma'am, I don't know who you are, but you might have just saved my life."

She looked at the marshal with steel-gray eyes, a pretty thing, Josh thought, were it not for the grim face. "I am Earlene Hanover. This man was my husband." She stepped nearer until she was standing over the body and staring at it.

Josh had moved next to the marshal now, and she turned and looked at the men, and he saw clearly the swollen face and fingerprint bruises and welts on her neck. She gave a sad close-lipped smile. "I guess this makes me a widow now. Somehow, I'm not grief-stricken. Of course, I must inform my children of their father's passing. Will I go to prison?"

Calder said, "Of course not, ma'am. You possibly saved the lives of law officers. You will need to stay in town a spell. There will be questions."

"Oh, dear. I should get home—that's in Illinois—to my children."

"Well, I..."

Josh interrupted. "Is that a Colt you're carrying, ma'am?"

"Yes. I carry it loaded and ready in my carpetbag."

"I carry a Colt," Josh said. "Chance, didn't you see me sneak up and take this man down?"

"Josh, no."

"This lady's got plenty of worries to deal with, and she shouldn't have to tell her kids she killed their father. There are three of us who know. Why don't we just make it easier for everybody. I'll write down a better statement for your records."

"You'll probably be a hero."

"That's a thought."

Calder said, "Ma'am go ahead and go home. You will have to come back for legal things here."

Josh said, "Your husband was a resident of this territory. I don't know what he had in the way of property, and considering the way it was acquired, there could be a lot of claims against it. A search should be made for a will, but I am betting against one turning up considering he was likely one of those who never figured on dying. In that case, as surviving spouse you will have priority to appointment as administrator of his estate or the authority to name somebody to take on that task."

"I don't want to deal with this. I must find a lawyer before I leave town."

Calder said, "Josh Rivers here is Santa Fe's best probate lawyer, ma'am."

She looked at Josh. "You're a lawyer? You certainly don't look like one."

"I've been told that before. I'm with Rivers and Sinclair."

"Would you take on this case—be the administrator, too?"

"I don't see why not. Why don't I send a buggy out for you at ten o'clock tomorrow morning? You can visit me at the office and talk about this."

She extended her hand, and he accepted her firm grip. "You are hired, and I will be awaiting the buggy, and thank you—for everything." She turned to the marshal. "Am I free to go?"

"Since you didn't kill anybody, I guess so."

She wheeled and walked away with a bounce in her step like a girl who had just been let out of school.

The men watched her go down the hall. Calder said, "I can't believe how you dang shysters weasel your ways into business. With all those claims out there, why would you even want this case?"

"Lawyer and administrator fees are priority claims that come before anything else."

Calder shook his head. "Why am I not surprised? Another question between you and me. Do you think she was going to kill the son-of-a-bitch even if we had not come along?"

"Yeah. I do."

Chapter 45

JAEL AND JOSH watched the buckboard head down the road with Michael driving the mule team and his cousin Katherine Rivers sitting too closely on the seat beside him. Her father, Nathan Rivers, rode alongside astride a big bay gelding. Jael fought back tears as her son left for the Slash R for the remainder of the summer. She was losing him to that darn ranch. She knew it and part of her was happy for him, but she was also sad about the physical distance that would someday be between them.

Nate and Katherine had spent the night as their guests, and she knew Josh had enjoyed a chance to talk to his brother at some length. She had enjoyed getting to know the pert and pretty Katherine better. She had to struggle to find anything to criticize the auburn-haired girl about except the bond she and Michael obviously shared. She just hoped they could keep a rein on that friendship. Maybe a long absence when summer ended would send them in other directions.

Josh's arm wrapped around her waist, and he pulled her close. "Michael will be back in a few months. Everything will be fine."

She sighed. "Yes, I'm sure it will, and I have a law practice to deal with and wedding details to work out. We do both need to go into the office this afternoon, you know."

"Yeah, I have another appointment with Earlene Hanover before she leaves on the train this afternoon. We couldn't come up with a will at the castle, but I didn't get a chance to tell you that we found the safe combination written in pencil on the underside of the desk. No legal papers in the safe but lots of money, much of it gold coins. Some record of bank accounts at other locations, too. I don't know what we'll turn up eventually. At least we know there is enough cash to pay the lawyers. If there is something left after claims, Earlene gets a third and the kids receive two-thirds. Of course, conservatorships for the assets will need to be set up for the kids till they are of legal age."

"And I wonder who the conservator might be."

"Well, I assured the client I would help wherever I could."

"Mister Helpful."

"I'm leaving for work."

They both turned to see Rylee coming out the door.

Jael said, "First day back. Nervous?"

"Oh, no. Excited. I can't wait. When Mister Spiegelberg was out to visit, he talked about so many things he wants to do with the bank in the future, and I didn't tell you, I am now the first person outside the Spiegelberg family to serve on the bank's board of directors. I am so lucky."

"And so competent," Jael said. "We need to talk about this wedding, too. We've got six days."

"Tonight, I promise. Gabe will come over, and we can sit down and discuss it. He really doesn't want anything to do with it but show up, but I am not letting him off that easily."

"Somehow that sounds familiar." She looked at Josh, and he rolled his eyes and shrugged.

"I am having lunch with Tabby and Jessica this noon," Rylee said. "Jessica's spirits were boosted by Tabby's report on the success of the 'British Blondes' show, and the troupe has agreed to return. Tabby is willing to be more involved at the theater and has agreed to write a script for a play to be performed there with the thought she would submit it to one of her publishers. And Oliver will paint some special scenery for it."

Rylee gave them both hugs. "It's so good to be back. I love you both. And, Josh, I'm counting on you to walk me down the two-row aisle."

She hurried off the veranda toward the stable, and Jael called after her, "Michael said he saddled your horse before he left."

Rylee waved and disappeared into the stable.

It was suddenly quiet, and they walked into the house to face more silence. Jael said, "It's not even nine o'clock yet. Do you suppose we should go on into the office? There's always work waiting on our desks."

"But we're alone."

"Yes, and what has that got to do with it?"

"Think about it. Alone. You can scream all you want, and nobody will hear."

"Now, if you keep needling me about that, you will be doing some screaming yourself, and it won't be the happy kind."

"Is that a 'yes?'"

She feigned annoyance. "That's a 'maybe.' It depends on whether you make it worthwhile."

He raised his right hand. "I promise."

"Said the shyster to the innocent maiden." But she was already unbuttoning her blouse and headed for the bedroom.

About the Author

Ron Schwab is the author of several popular Western series, including *The Blood Hounds*, *Lockwood*, *The Coyote Saga*, and *The Lockes*. His novels *Grit* and *Old Dogs* were both awarded the Western Fictioneers Peacemaker Award for Best Western Novel, and Cut Nose was a finalist for the Western Writers of America Best Western Historical Novel.

Ron and his wife, Bev, divide their time between their home in Fairbury, Nebraska and their cabin in the Kansas Flint Hills.

For more information about Ron Schwab and his books, you may visit the author's website at www.ronschwabbooks.com.